MW00778371

THE AMISH SPINSTER

AMISH MISFITS BOOK 2 (AMISH ROMANCE)

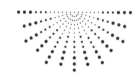

SAMANTHA PRICE

CHAPTER ONE

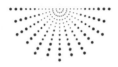

*L*ydia Raber was happy most of the time. She'd be much happier if it weren't for her mother's constant nagging about her getting out more and mixing with others like her sisters. They went to all the singings, the volleyball games and whatever else the young people did. Why couldn't her mother understand that at twenty-five, she was past all of that? There was nothing worse than being the oldest person at the young-peoples' events, and always being thought of as one of the youth organizers even though she wasn't.

When she heard a buggy on a chilly Saturday afternoon, Lydia got up from her bed where she'd been taking a nap. Tugging her quilt with her, she looked out the window as she wrapped it around herself.

The sister closest to her in age, Paula, had returned from a buggy ride with Winston. Winston Yoder was a nice young man and got on so well with Paula that Sarah, their youngest sister, and Lydia thought the two would marry. That was about the only thing Sarah and she agreed on. Like many younger sisters, Sarah was so often a nuisance. Pulling the warmth of the feather-stuffed quilt higher around her neck, and simply out of curiosity, she kept a quiet eye on Paula and Winston. She had so few things to amuse herself these days.

From the upstairs window, she stared at

them as closely as her old barn cat would silently watch birds at play. Just like her cat knew he would never be fast enough to catch the prey, Lydia knew that love was just as much out of her reach. Still, that didn't stop her from watching the two lovebirds. Paula did her own special love dance of laughing, chattering and fluttering of eyelashes. Winston responded with laughter and a tender touch on Paula's arm.

Tiger, the barn cat, suddenly appeared at the barn door, apparently sensing someone was thinking about him, or perhaps it was dinnertime? Yes, that would be more likely. He sauntered slowly past the couple in love as though they didn't exist, and continued toward the house.

Winston now had his arm up, leaning on the back of his buggy, while Paula stood as close as she could without actually touching him. Every now and again, he'd say something that made Paula giggle. Whatever two people in love talked about was a mystery to Lydia. She could see from Paula's sparkling eyes how much she was in love. Paula would say something, and then Winston would say something back and she'd laugh. It was a recurring theme.

The jokes and chattering ended and now they were serious; the smiles and laughter had been replaced with staring deep into each other's eyes.

Envy filled Lydia's heart and she closed her eyes, imagining she was looking into someone's handsome face and giggling at something he'd said. She was snapped from her daydream when she realized she was too old for girlish giggles and too large to be cute. That carefree heart was something that only teenagers had, and she was well past that.

There was a gap of seven years between Paula and herself, and nine years between herself and Sarah. She'd often reasoned the gap in age was due to her parents being reluctant to have another child any sooner due to shock when she slithered out of the womb. She'd been told she held the record for the largest baby born in the county.

Her birth had been painful for her mother and must've given her father a fright. It was fine for a boy to be big, but for a girl to be born a fraction shy of fourteen pounds seemed wrong.

Lydia was born big and stayed that way. Even as a child she'd towered over children her own age and had always been mistaken for someone much older. It wasn't fair that she was the only one in the family burdened by her appearance. Many people had told Lydia that God had meant her to look the way she did. The purpose of looking that way eluded her. There was no possible reason as far as she could ascertain; it had only ever made her miserable. Surely God didn't want His children to be despondent? What purpose did it serve God for her to tower so tall over all the other women in the community? And many of the men, too?

She wiped the fogged up window with the edge of the quilt and continued her envious thoughts even though she knew it was wrong to have envy in her heart.

Envy intensified when Paula giggled loud enough for it to be heard through the bedroom window. As quickly as she could, Lydia pushed those feelings out of her heart. Her sisters couldn't help the way they looked any more than she could help the way she was. She had to be happy for her sisters; she wouldn't wish her looks on them or anyone.

"What are you doing?"

Lydia jumped away from the window and stared at Sarah. "Nothing."

Sarah rushed to the window and looked outside. Seeing the lovebirds, she whipped her head around and stared up into Lydia's face. "You're *spying* on them!"

"I wasn't. I was just looking out the window."

"You were spying. Wait until I tell *Mamm*."

"*Nee*, don't."

"What's it worth?"

Lydia opened her mouth in shock. Although she shouldn't have been surprised; it had become Sarah's way lately to bargain for everything.

"Your dessert tonight?" she asked.

"I'll tell *Mamm* you came into my room without knocking again. She told you only yesterday to respect my privacy."

"Paula doesn't mind if I go into *her* room without knocking."

"Well, I do."

Sarah plonked herself onto Lydia's bed. "I reckon you want Winston for yourself."

Lydia laughed. "He's way too young."

"You're jealous because you don't have a boyfriend."

Lydia looked down at the young couple once more. Knowing Sarah wouldn't expect such a response, she said, *"Jah,* I guess you're right. It might be nice to have a boyfriend."

"Well, you could get one, too, if you wanted, Lydia."

Lydia nodded and then gave a little shrug.

"You could," Sarah insisted.

Now looking at the wide-eyed Sarah, she asked, "You think so?"

"Jah, but then you'd have to marry after that."

"I'd like that. As long as it's the right man."

Sarah screwed up her face.

Seeing Sarah's scowl, Lydia said, "You'll change your mind when you get older."

"I'll think about that later. Anyway, if you don't like anyone here, why don't you travel and stay with Aunt Stella? *Dat* said you could go stay there. She's never married."

Lydia remembered a conversation the other night over dinner. Her mother suggested she travel around and see a few other communities. She knew her mother was thinking she might meet a man. Lydia laughed. "Remember when we visited Aunt Stella and she gave us that strange drink? She called it Tooti Frooti."

"*Jah*. I threw mine in the bushes when she wasn't looking."

"Me too. It was dreadful. I don't even know how I remember the name. It's been burned into my brain, I guess."

"She seems old fashioned and everything, but that's because she's old. I remember that she seemed kind."

"That's true."

"Anyway, when you leave here can I have this room?" Sarah asked.

"I'm not going anywhere. Anyway, what's wrong with yours?"

Sarah got off the bed and looked out the window standing right beside Lydia. "Yours has got a much better view. And you can see right up and down the road in both directions. I'd know who was coming to the *haus* before anyone else."

"Hmm. That'd be up to *Mamm* and *Dat,* but I don't mind. If I'm not here, it won't matter to me. I think I'll always be here, though." When she saw Sarah's sad face, she said, "Sorry to disappoint you."

"You should go away—go traveling, I mean, like *Mamm* said."

"You just want my room."

"*Jah,* I do." Sarah giggled. Then she looked down at Winston and Paula. "Do you think they might kiss?"

"*Nee,* I don't think so. Not until she's chosen him to marry."

"She's in love with him. Look at the way

she's acting, all silly. They'll get married before you do."

That had already occurred to Lydia. Her younger sister marrying before she did would be dreadful. Then a year or two after that, Sarah would marry, and then what would become of her? It was a frightening thing to think about. When she was younger, she thought love just happened and she always thought someone would come along, but no one ever did.

"Maybe they will marry before me," Lydia muttered quietly in answer to Sarah's previous comment.

"Will that make you upset?" Her sister stared into her face.

She couldn't admit that it would, or Sarah would make a fuss over it and tell their mother and tell Paula. "I wouldn't know how I'd feel until it happened. Has he asked her yet? Have they talked about getting married?"

Sarah shrugged her shoulders. "She never talks to me anymore now that she's got Winston to talk to. Now she says I'm annoying and I'm crowding her space."

Lydia looked out the window. "I'd say they will marry. It's only a matter of time."

"What about Ed Byler?"

"What about him?"

"You know, for you? To marry?"

"Oh, Ed's too young. He's twenty-two and I'm twenty-five. I'd need a man older than I am, and taller."

Sarah shook her head. "There aren't many taller than you are."

"*Ach, denke* for reminding me."

Sarah stood on her tiptoes reaching as high as she could. "I wish I was as tall as you are. Then I'd leave the Amish and become a supermodel."

Lydia laughed. "Well, you wouldn't want to be tall, and heavy too, like I am. Supermodel's are skinny and definitely not big-boned like me."

"*Nee.* I'd want to be tall and skinny. Anyway, you're not fat or anything."

"You don't think so?"

"*Nee.*"

"I feel it."

"Well, you're not. Not at all."

Both her sisters were average height and she stood six feet tall. She used to stoop her shoulders until one time she was in town and caught sight of her reflection in one of the store windows. It was then she knew that standing straight was preferable over stooping, which made her look as though she had an affliction. She wanted to feel feminine but rarely did because of her large size.

As her dear little sister had just pointed out, there weren't many men in the community who were taller than she was, and that was on her secret list of 'must haves' in a man.

He had to be taller and, ideally, never married before. The last thing she wanted was to marry a man and look after his children. Her cousin Alana had married a widower and now she was miserable. She'd told Lydia in confidence that she was sure that he only married her to have someone to care for the children and the house, and he hardly paid her any mind.

She would not have a marriage of convenience; better to have no marriage than a marriage without love. Whatever Paula felt in her heart when she looked at Winston, that was something that Lydia wanted to experience.

"Anyway, *Mamm* told me to fetch you to help with dinner," Sarah said.

Lydia frowned at her youngest sister. "Why didn't you say so?"

"I just did."

Unwinding the bed quilt from her shoulders, Lydia said, "Right away, I mean. I didn't realize it was getting so late in the day."

"That's what happens when you spy on people, time just flies."

Lydia spread her quilt back over her bed and walked toward the door shaking her head at Sarah. "Just don't tell anyone I was looking out the window. Okay?"

"Hmm, only if I can have your share of pie tonight."

"Sarah, that's extortion," Lydia whispered as they started down the stairs.

"I believe it's actually bribery. Money changes hands with extortion, if I'm not wrong."

Lydia giggled. "What did they teach you at *schul?*"

"I overhear things at the bakery."

"That sort of things? Some bakery! Okay. You can have my pie just this once. Anyway, don't you see enough pies at the bakery?"

"You can never get too much pie."

If Lydia had been thinner, smaller, she would've had the confidence to get a job like her sisters had done. Paula worked at the farmers markets and Sarah worked at a bakery.

A change had to be made in her life. Lydia knew she couldn't go on any longer the way things were. The last thing she wanted was for another year to pass and things to remain exactly the same.

CHAPTER TWO

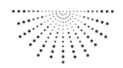

*L*ydia walked into the kitchen and saw their mother stirring something on the stove. "*Mamm.* I'm sorry but I didn't notice the time was going so quickly."

Sarah, who was right behind her, said, "Lydia was too busy looking out the window."

Their mother turned around. "What were you looking at, Lydia?"

Lydia glared at Sarah, who didn't stop

there. "She was spying on Winston and Paula."

Their mother glared at Sarah. "Sarah, mind your tongue."

"I was. Well, I suppose I wasn't, but it's hard to keep quiet sometimes."

"That's why you need to learn some self-discipline," their mother told Sarah. Then she turned to Lydia. "What's so interesting about Winston and Paula?"

Sarah piped up, "They're in love, that's what's so interesting about them."

"Jah," Lydia said. "And that's something I know nothing about." She thought she might as well say it because if she didn't, Sarah would.

"Perhaps you should take up my suggestion of visiting relations. I've always said that if you pray you must also take action. Faith without works is dead, and you know that."

Lydia nodded, slightly annoyed that her mother had an answer for everything and often quoted scriptures at her to prove her points. "Who do you think I should visit?"

"Your *vadder* and I were discussing that you should visit his *schweschder,* your Aunt Stella."

"We were just talking about her weren't we, Lydia?"

"Yes, we were." Lydia had to wonder whether her mother also discussed her single status with her friends went she went to the quilting bees. She hoped she wasn't their topic of conversation. She could almost hear them saying, *Poor Lydia needs a husband. If she doesn't get one now it'll only get harder for her to find someone. Doesn't she like any of the available men around here?*

The thing was that the available men were young men around Winston's age, or older widowers, and not one of them tall. None of them appealed to her and she was sure she didn't appeal to them either.

Lydia's mother jolted her from her daydreams. "I'll have your *vadder* call her tomorrow and see if you could stay with her. It could just be a quick visit. You only need stay a week or so. Have a look around and see if any of the men there suit you."

Lydia looked at her younger sister. "Will you come with me?"

"I can't. I've got work and I couldn't ask for the time off when I've only just started."

"I suppose I could stay with her if she doesn't mind—if I won't be in the way."

Her mother smiled. "I'm sure she'd love it if you stayed."

Lydia knew that she had to get out and make something happen. How would she find a man if she didn't? Sure, she could wait around for a suitable man to come visiting, maybe at a wedding or a funeral, but she'd never even met a man at one of those things in the last few years, suitable or otherwise, so why would the next few years be any different?

The three of them in the kitchen all turned when Paula walked in the back door.

"Isn't Winston staying for dinner again tonight?" Sarah asked.

"Nee not tonight. He said he would wear out his welcome if he was here again tonight."

When Sarah opened her mouth to say something, Lydia glared at her and, thankfully, Sarah thought better of it and closed her mouth. Lydia knew she'd been going to say something about him being there every night for dinner for the past two weeks. And Sarah had probably been about to say just how many dinners he'd had there.

Instead of talking about Winston, Lydia became the topic of conversation when Sarah said, "Lydia is going off to Aunt Stella's to find a husband."

"Sarah, I don't want people to think that. I'll merely be visiting just to look at the community and to have a change of scenery."

Their mother said, "She's always asking for you girls to stay with her, but it's not easy now with both of you having jobs," she said, looking at Sarah and Paula.

Sarah said, "Lydia said I could have her room when she moves out."

"That's not fair! I want that room. It's bigger and better and that's where the morning sun hits," Paula said.

"Too bad for you, I asked first and anyway you'll be getting married soon, won't you?"

Hushed silence fell over the room, and all eyes were on Paula.

"He hasn't said anything about marriage, so I don't know."

"Are you sure he hasn't said anything?" Sarah asked with her chin tilted high.

"*Nee.* If he'd said something I would tell you because we'd have a lot of arrangements to make."

"That's right. I'd need plenty of notice," their mother said, turning back to the stove.

"I think I'll never have a wedding or get married," Sarah said. "I don't want to do the same things as everyone else."

"Nonsense, Sarah, I don't know why you keep coming out with such strange things. You'll have a wedding just like everybody else in the community. Now sit down and shell those peas, they won't shell themselves you know."

During their dinner of roasted pork with vegetables and sauerkraut, Lydia's mother raised the subject of Aunt Stella.

"Good idea," Lydia's father said. "How do you feel about staying there for a while, Lydia?"

"I suppose that's best."

Her father put his knife and fork down and stared at his oldest daughter for a moment. "Well, you don't look too happy about the idea."

She was a little embarrassed to tell her father that she knew she had to do something to find a husband. "I would like to stay with her. I haven't seen her for years. And I don't have a job yet, so I'm free to do things like that. As long as you don't mind being left with all the chores, *Mamm?*"

"You enjoy yourself. I've got Sarah and Paula here to help me."

"*Jah,* but what if Paula gets married soon? Then I'll have to do all the work myself."

Everyone laughed.

"You don't have many chores to do," their father said to Sarah.

"*Nee,* but it's a lot when I work at the bakery and have to come home and do chores, and then I have to do chores before I leave in the morning as well."

"Welcome to the real world," Paula said to Sarah.

Sarah pulled a face at Paula and then got into trouble from their mother.

CHAPTER THREE

*L*ydia stepped onto the train and quickly moved to claim a window seat. The streaks of rain that fell down the windows made Lydia wish that she was listening to the rain while lying in her own bed. It was a bothersome thing to have to put in so much effort to find a man, when Paula had found one in their own community. Maybe if she looked more like Paula a man would've gravitated to her. While not considering herself exactly ugly, Lydia knew she had many flaws. Firstly there was her height, and that would've been fine, or at least not so bad, if she'd had a slender frame.

Not once had she met a man who truly liked her for herself.

At twenty-five years-of-age, Lydia was reaching the point of no return. Single Amish women her age were often left on the shelf and never married. That's where Aunt Stella would come in. Lydia's parents had mulled over the decision for some time, but as it became clear that Lydia had been unable to attract a man, they had gotten in touch with Aunt Stella who knew many people and lived in Allentown. She was always telling Lydia's parents there were many single men there and the three girls should visit.

Aunt Stella had gone so far as to assure Lydia's parents that she'd find Lydia a suitable husband in no time at all, since she was heavily involved in Amish social circles and had connections with those in neighboring communities as well. Those things still weren't enough to make Lydia optimistic, but it was far too late to focus on the negatives now. The train vibrated and then came to life as it rumbled away from the station, taking her to uncertainty.

In her younger days so many men had overlooked her for a pretty face and a slender frame. It annoyed Lydia that men wouldn't wait to get to know her before they passed her by. Didn't they know that looks fade and what's on the inside lasts forever?

When it gets so bad that you have to leave home just so you can have a chance at finding a husband, that's when you know that life has turned its back on you.

Staring through the rain-spattered windows, Lydia couldn't help but see sadness in the gray skies. The trees were bare, their branches stretching high into the pale sky as a dreary storm painted the world in muted depressing shades. It was almost as though the sky and all the angels in heaven were weeping for her, which at least gave her a little comfort.

The suggestion from her parents that she go to Aunt Stella's was just as much for their benefit as it was for hers; she was sure about that. With her gone, they could concentrate on her younger sisters. Surely Paula was soon to marry Winston Yoder.

Slouching further into her seat, Lydia noticed a small boy staring in her direction. His scrunched brow and tilted head spoke volumes, and his gaze stayed upon her for much longer than was polite. Then he whispered to his mother who glanced over at Lydia and then she whispered in his ear. He was asking why that lady was so big, Lydia was certain of that. Or was he staring because of her Amish clothing? She hoped his mother told him that it wasn't right to stare at people.

To take her mind off of such things during the tiresome trip, Lydia pulled out a newspaper that her father had given her for the ride. He had always been trying to get her to read the Amish newspapers, but there wasn't much news in them. Just notes of who was visiting whom, and birth and death notices of people she didn't even know. A long trip alone was the perfect time to get lost in some reading, though, and make up stories in her mind about what these people were like.

As she read about various things, like farming or the latest plow inventions, she could feel someone staring. Looking up, she noticed it was that boy again.

Lydia stopped reading and folded her newspaper up neatly. Then, she slowly glared over at the boy, and his mother whispered to him again. Folding her arms across her chest, Lydia closed her eyes. She was relieved when she opened them at the next stop to see the woman and the boy getting off the train.

Even though Lydia was slightly daunted about meeting the men her aunt spoke of, she was excited at the thought of seeing Aunt Stella again. Maybe her aunt *could* use her influence and personal knowledge to find a suitable man who would look past her appearance and take the time to get to know her.

Finally, she was at her destination, but that wasn't the end of this; it was just the beginning.

After pulling into the station, the doors of the train were pulled open and the passengers all poured out like a river through a broken dam. Standing alone in a sea of strangers, Lydia looked around for a familiar face. Then, her aunt stepped through the crowd. With both arms outstretched, she brought her niece into a tight hug.

"How was your trip?"

"*Gut, denke.*"

"Is that your only bag?"

Lydia glanced down at the bag she was holding. "*Jah,* that's all I brought with me."

CHAPTER FOUR

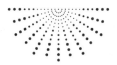

*L*ydia was exhausted from the long train ride, but she wasn't done traveling just yet. Aunt Stella lived farther from the train station than she'd expected and she warned Lydia the taxi ride would be a long one. Her aunt took no time getting to the heart of the matter; after all, it was the entire reason she was there.

"I've already arranged for a few people to come to dinner tomorrow night. Since it is a gloomy day today, that ended up working out perfectly," she said, talking more to herself now than to Lydia. She must have realized it too, because she quickly shook her head and glanced at her niece. "Anyway, I've gotten in touch with my friends and have set up a rather nice get-together for tomorrow night. There will also be young men there for you to meet."

There might be plenty of men there, but how many of them would want me? Lydia wondered, sighing to herself at the thought. "Sounds lovely," she said, trying to avoid eye-contact with her aunt.

"It should be, my dear. I know you're under a lot of scrutiny as of late, but I believe I can help you. I've already worked on a plan to find you a special husband."

"He doesn't need to be anything special. A nice and kind man is all I need."

Aunt Stella laughed. "Then that's what we'll find you."

When Lydia got to Aunt Stella's home, Stella showed her through the house.

Aunt Stella's house was a sparsely furnished and small two-bedroom home. It was neat and tidy. Rather than bare floorboards with rugs, all of the floors were covered in cream-colored linoleum. Lydia wondered how the floors fared in the cooler weather. Perhaps she might be there long enough to find out. Upstairs were two bedrooms, and a third room that Stella used as her sewing room. Lydia supposed it might have made a small third bedroom if a family lived there. In the center of the room was a table for cutting out fabrics and patterns, and in the corner of the room was a treadle sewing machine. It was old fashioned compared to the gas-powered one that Lydia used at home.

Looking out the window, Lydia admired the view across the countryside. "You can see for miles from here."

"*Jah,* I like sitting here sewing. Mind you, I don't have much chance to look out at it when I'm on the machine."

The next room was Stella's. "This room's the same size as yours."

"That's a beautiful quilt with all those stars."

"*Jah,* it was the same pattern as my *mudder* had many years ago, but it burned up in a *haus* fire. That would've been your *grossmammi.*"

"*Dat* told me nothing about a fire. I hope no one was hurt."

"*Nee.* It happened when we children were young and all of us were out at a meeting. Your *Dat* would've only been about five then, so he might not remember much. It's an odd sensation to have only what you stand up in. We all stayed at a neighbor's *haus* until ours was rebuilt."

"I must ask him about those stories when I get home. Surely he'd remember something of it. Something that scary had to make an impression, even if he was young."

"Your *vadder* isn't much of a talker."

"I know. But if I ask him about it, he'll surely tell me something."

Looking back at the quilt, she said, "I always remembered my *mudder's* quilt. When I got older, I made one just the same, as best I could recall, and gave it to her."

"She would've loved that."

"Jah, she cried. She said her *mudder*-in-law, and all the women in the *familye* had made it for her, and they gave it to her on her wedding day."

Wedding Day! That made Lydia wonder again if she'd ever have one of those.

"And your room is here, right next door."

Lydia stepped into the room. It was dark with the curtains drawn. Taking a few steps, Lydia pulled the curtains apart and got a view of the barn. The bedroom was located in the same position as hers at home. "It's a lovely view."

"Jah. Now let's get some food into you."

Stella left the room and Lydia followed. "I thought we'd have chicken and vegetables."

"I love chicken," Lydia said as she walked down the stairs behind her aunt.

"Now, while I'm cooking would you like some Tooti Frooti?"

"Um, no thanks. I had a lot to drink on the train."

"Cup of hot tea then?"

"*Jah,* that would be lovely."

"Then after dinner you can unpack your belongings."

THE NEXT MORNING, Lydia woke with a churning sensation in her stomach. She told herself it was just nerves. All she could think about was the dinner her aunt had arranged for that night. Knowing that things might not be any better amongst the men in this town, she fell into a pit of despair. Tears flowed down her cheeks. Letting her tears fall into the pillow, she wanted to scream. When she had cried until she could cry no more, she sat up and sighed loudly. The problem was she'd been whispered about so much and received so many stares she found it hard not to feel rejected before she even met anyone.

What was she going to wear? Her aunt had told her to wear her Sunday-best, but the only suitable dress she had brought with her was tight and looked it.

After sobbing quietly in her room for some time, a gentle knock sounded on her door. "Lydia? Are you okay? I haven't seen you yet this morning, and I heard some strange noises coming from in there."

Startled, Lydia quickly sat up and rolled out of bed. She wiped away the remnants of her tears before pulling the door open. "I'm fine, Aunt Stella. It's just that I'm tired from the long trip," she said.

Aunt Stella opened her door wider and peeped in. "Oh, well, you look rather sad. Please be honest with me. Is something wrong?"

Lydia sighed again, realizing that she had been caught in a lie. "Well, I *am* fine; it's just that I don't know what I'm going to wear tonight. The only dress I used to wear for Sunday-best no longer fits. But I don't have another option. I've nothing I would call a best dress."

Aunt Stella put her hands on her hips and shook her head. "You've put on weight?"

"*Jah.* And I'm so tall. I don't want to be tall and fat."

"You're not fat at all, you're quite normal for your frame. You've got to think about yourself differently."

She was surprised to hear her aunt say such a thing.

Her aunt continued, "You're never going to find the man you deserve unless you believe you deserve him. It's just the way the world works."

Lydia didn't know what to say, but her chest was so tight that something as simple as breathing became difficult. "Okay," she muttered, turning back to her bed. As soon as her aunt left the room she would eat that chocolate bar she had in her bag. Times like this called for one thing, and one thing only, and that was comfort. It was just an unfortunate thing that sometimes her comfort came in the form of food.

"How about I make you a dress today? I'm a fast sewer. We'll head into town and I'll buy some material and we can sew one in no time at all."

"Really? Oh, Aunt Stella, that would be so nice of you. Are you certain?" Lydia wouldn't feel so self-conscious in a larger dress.

"I'm more than happy to do that. Surely I can spoil you a little since I don't have daughters of my own, *jah?*"

"Denke."

"A new dress and a fresh start is what you need." She pointed toward Lydia's clothes. "Now get dressed and we can leave after breakfast." Aunt Stella left her alone to change.

Having a new dress wasn't the answer to all of her problems, but at least she'd have something nice to wear. She would make the best of her appearance and try not to worry about what the night might bring. The only way that life was going to improve for her was if she listened to her aunt and did everything in her power to better herself. Her aunt had done well for herself, and she had a happy life even though she had no children and had never married.

After they'd had their breakfast, they traveled to the main part of town where the stores lined both sides of the wide street.

"I'm taking you to the best fabric store in town."

Lydia's throat tightened. *"Mamm* refused to let me make any more dresses until I lost some of my weight, but I didn't."

"You look fine. Men don't like women who are stick thin, with their bones sticking out. I know how you young girls can be, so if it bothers you, walking is what you need to do. We'll set about having you take a brisk walk every morning."

Lydia nodded, wishing now that she had kept her mouth closed. She hated walking.

Aunt Stella pointed to the fabric shop as they approached it. It was a two level building with windows either side of the front door.

Vibrant red fabric in the window caught Lydia's eye. "Aunt Stella, look at that red material."

Aunt Stella shook her head before she even looked at it. "You know we don't wear red, and even if we did, you'd stand out far too much."

After looking around for several minutes, Aunt Stella picked out several colors she liked. Apart from the forbidden red, Lydia liked all the pale colors, the yellows, and the soft greens.

"Those colors won't do. You need darker colors so you'll appear smaller."

"But older women wear these dark colors." Older women, like ones her mother's age.

"When you lose the weight, you can wear the lighter colors. That is, if you're serious about wanting to look slimmer."

"Jah, I am."

"Well, which is it?"

"I'll go for the darker ones."

Her aunt wasn't giving her a choice. She was bossy. Lydia's father had often referred to her in a joking way as his 'bossy older *schweschder,'* but Lydia could now see the truth in his words.

Why couldn't she be slim like her sisters?

They'd taken after their slender mother, whereas she'd taken after her large-framed father.

"Lydia, just choose something. If you don't, we won't have time to make it before tonight."

"*Jah*, I'm trying, but everything I like, you don't."

The sales assistant pointed out a dark grape shade. "How about this one?" she asked. "Many young people like this color, and it's dark."

It wasn't too bad. Lydia turned to her aunt. "What do you think?"

Her aunt pushed her lips out. "Could be worse. Get that if you want."

Lydia turned to the sales woman. "We'll take three yards of that one, thank you."

The sales assistant pulled out the roll of material from the rack. "Have a look at it against your skin in the mirror before you decide."

Lydia recoiled. Mirror? She hated mirrors. They all made her look much bigger than she really was. "No, that's okay. I'm sure it will look good."

The sales woman, nearly as bossy as her aunt, held the material roll in one hand and with the other she pulled Lydia toward a full-length mirror. Lydia had no choice but to look at herself in her old dress—the one that fitted best—while the lady pulled out the fabric and held it against her body.

Stella had followed them and now peered over Lydia's shoulder. "I've things to do. I can't be here all day. Get that and make do."

"Don't you think it suits her?" the woman asked Stella.

"*Jah,* I do."

"Thank you. I'll take it," Lydia said for the third time.

"I think that one looks better than the others by far." The assistant gave a self-satisfied smile as she took the roll of fabric to the cutting table.

Lydia agreed, and smiled. It didn't look amazing, but it did look passable and it was a vast improvement on what the others had been. Not feeling confident about the night to come, she was at least pleased she'd have something nice to wear if Stella and she could sew it in time, as well as prepare the food for the meal.

"Denke, Aunt Stella." Lydia threw her arms around her aunt's neck.

Stella leaned back as though she'd never been hugged before. Then she gave Lydia a little pat on her back. "You're welcome, my dear."

CHAPTER FIVE

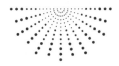

Stella and Lydia had sewed from the time they got home until a couple of hours before the guests were due. At various times throughout the day they'd baked the beef and the chicken. When they'd finally finished the dress, they both spent the next hours on the meal. Lydia's first job was to peel all the potatoes for mashing, while Stella turned her attention to the dessert pies. The previous day she'd prepared the crusts, and that left her to fill the crusts with apple and rhubarb. When everything had been done in the kitchen except for making the gravy, Lydia rushed up the stairs to pull on her new dress and get ready.

Minutes later, she heard footsteps coming up the steps. "My dear niece, are you ready yet?" her aunt said, calling out from the other side of her bedroom door.

"Just a few more minutes." Lydia frantically worked the brush through her thick tangled hair. She was at least an hour away from looking good, but time was ticking away and there were only a few minutes before the guests were to arrive. After doing her best in the amount of time she had, Lydia pulled the door open to see Aunt Stella standing there.

She had a smile on her face, but behind her compassionate eyes hid the truth. "You look lovely, my dear," she said, gently nudging Lydia toward the front door. "There will be two nice young men here tonight. Perhaps if you open the door for them it'll be good."

"Okay, but how will I know which men are single?"

"Oh, you'll certainly know. They'll arrive alone, of course."

The first guests to arrive were two young men, Albie and John. Albie was tall with light reddish colored hair and a face full of freckles, and he spoke loudly. Between the two men, he was the more outgoing. John was dark-haired and a little shorter than Lydia. First impressions were that neither one of these men was suitable, but if she didn't want to be subject to first impressions she knew she had to give the men the same chance.

A little after the two young men had arrived, the house quickly filled with older couples. Lydia had expected her aunt to invite some single woman too, and since she hadn't, it seemed an obvious setup that the two men had been invited so Stella could find a match for her niece. In a less than subtle ploy, Aunt Stella sat Lydia in between the two young men. Albie did most of the talking, asking Lydia where she was from, how many were in her family, and why she was staying with her aunt.

She answered that she was staying at Aunt Stella's to have a little vacation before she started work. And then she asked some questions of her own before Albie asked her what kind of job she was about to start since a job was only something she'd given vague thought to. Whenever she could, she jumped up to help Stella serve courses and help with the meal.

Rather than being an enjoyable night, Lydia had found it rather stressful. John had been hard to get to know, and Albie had talked so loud that it made her head hurt.

When the last of the guests had left, Stella

closed the door and turned to face Lydia. "What did you think of them?"

"They seem nice, but neither of them is for me."

"You have to get to know someone a little better before you can just say they don't suit you."

Lydia had no response and turned her attention to the coffee cups that now littered the living room and set about gathering them up. *"Denke* for tonight, Aunt Stella. I really appreciate all the efforts you're going to for me."

"Don't change the subject. Tell me what was wrong with both of those young men, as you see it."

Lydia sighed at the way her aunt was challenging her.

Aunt Stella walked over and sat down on the couch. "Leave the cups and saucers where they are and sit down by me."

Lydia sat next to her aunt. "As I said, they

seem very nice. But John is just too quiet for me, and Albie is the opposite. She knew her aunt would be horrified if she also said that John was shorter and Albie was too noisy and neither of their personalities attracted her.

"I guess I'll just be like you, Aunt Stella. You're happy, aren't you?"

"I'm happy now because I know I will never be married. But you're so young, and you've got your whole life in front of you. I don't want you to miss out on the things that I missed out on. I don't have that one special person in my life, and I want that for you."

"But what if it just never happens for me? *Gott* might want me to stay single."

"If you believe, it will happen."

"Well, didn't you believe you'd find a husband?" She hoped she wasn't overstepping her boundaries asking such prying questions, but it's something she needed to know.

"I don't think I even prayed about it; it's just something that I expected to happen." Aunt Stella shrugged her shoulders and smiled. "If I did pray about it back then, I probably left things too long. All I want for you is to be happy."

Lydia smiled at her kindly aunt. "Why don't you go to bed, Aunt Stella? I'll do the washing up. You must be tired, with doing most of the cooking tonight and sewing all day."

"*Nee,* we'll do it together. One thing I've missed is companionship, and it's already been lovely having you here, so I want to make the most of it."

"Okay." Lydia rose to her feet. "I just can't look at these dishes any longer." She gathered as many up in her hands as she could and took them to the kitchen followed close behind by Aunt Stella, who had her hands full, too.

"Do you think Albie or John liked you?"

"Nee, only as a friend." Lydia stacked the dishes on the counter to the side of the sink.

"How can you be so sure?"

"Believe me, I've had enough experience to know what someone thinks about me." Lydia squirted detergent in the sink and turned on the hot water, carefully setting cups into the sudsy water. "They both in- vited me to a pizza night that's on soon. Just as a friend. It was nice of them."

Aunt Stella shook her head solemnly, picked up a tea towel and let out a drawn- out sigh. "I knew this was going to happen. It's a good thing I took other steps."

Lydia paused her mental torment just long enough to respond out of curiosity. "What other steps? What do you mean?"

"Turn the water off and come with me."

She turned the water off, dried her hands, and followed her aunt back into the living room.

"What is it?" Lydia asked.

Without answering right away, her aunt walked over to the desk and pulled a small stack of letters from it. "Here, read these and take your pick. Perhaps if you respond, you'll find a man who isn't like the others."

"What are these?" Lydia asked, as she accepted the letters from her aunt.

"As I said, I had a feeling that this would happen, so I wrote to a few people I know from other communities. Many of my women friends have sons your age. These are the letters that I've gotten back so far."

Her first instinct was to refuse, because she was certain that no man would want her when they saw her.

"What did you write to them about me? What did you tell them?"

"I said I had a single niece in her mid twenties looking to marry, and who was willing to move for love."

Had her aunt mentioned the fact that she was a larger woman than the average?

Aunt Stella nodded to the letters. "Read what they say about their sons."

"Oh, I can't read your letters."

"These aren't from my friends. They are from the men my friends found for you."

"Oh, really?" She was amazed that her aunt hadn't mentioned it when she'd first arrived. It seemed she didn't have much confidence in the content of the letters, or maybe she thought either John or Albie would've suited her and the letters wouldn't have needed to be read.

"Go on. That's the only way you'll get a true feeling for each one of them. Then, we'll talk tomorrow. If you'd like to meet any of these men, we'll set about arranging it."

"You've been so kind to me. I've never had anyone be so nice or care about me so much." She gave her aunt a quick kiss on her cheek. "I'll read them in my room after we've finished washing the dishes."

Aunt Stella gave a little chuckle. "I hope you find a nice man."

"Me too. *Denke.*" Her aunt certainly had taken on her problem as her own, just as her father had assured her that his sister would.

CHAPTER SIX

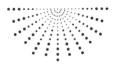

*L*ydia returned to her bedroom and got undressed, changing into her nightgown. The entire day had been more of a nightmare than a happily-ever-after, but that was how it always seemed to go for her. Hopeful that there might be a letter from her future husband among the ones from her aunt, she unbraided her hair and climbed into bed. As she lay there, she looked over the five letters while wondering which to read first.

"Here we go," she mumbled, shaking her

head. "This should be entertaining if nothing else."

The first letter was from a man who had gone to Canada to start a community and was looking for a wife to help him. Lydia mentally discarded that one before she'd even finished. She'd read it another time and make a polite response, but this was not the man for her. She didn't want to live a life of struggling in a small community in some cold harsh place. "Well, that one is definitely not going to happen," she uttered, tucking it back into its envelope before moving on to the next.

When she pulled out the second letter, Lydia immediately noticed plain large handwriting. The man was from a community near Ohio and all he said was that he was looking for a wife. There wasn't much information about his personality or his background. The next letters were much the same.

Aware that none of these men knew about her size, she gently folded the letters and opened the last letter. While she opened it, she thought about how these poor men had written under a false impression, thinking they were writing to an average-looking woman.

The last letter was from a man who owned an Amish business and who had recently lost his wife. He said he needed to fill the hole that she'd left. His words invoked sympathy, but he wasn't the right man for her. He'd surely compare her to his late wife, and that was a certain recipe for disaster. That letter went back into its envelope, too. She reread the other three letters again and chose the man who seemed the best suited.

Something inside Lydia wanted her to be honest and write about her height and weight, but then she heard her aunt's voice whispering in her ear. *Just tell them who you are and let them decide what they think based on that. Everything else will fall into place. There's no reason to list your flaws, since we all have them.* There was truth to the words she imagined her aunt saying.

She had no choice but to follow her aunt's advice and write back to the one she'd chosen. It was either that or go home and live at her parents house forever – a large and lonely spinster left on the shelf. Lydia prayed for the first time in days. She asked God to bring her a man who would love her just how she was. This is how God had made her; she knew God accepted her, and if He did, then someone with a good heart would too.

Pushing her reservations aside, Lydia pulled paper from her stationery set and made a quick response to each of the four "No thank you" letters before she responded to the most important one.

Lydia spent the next hour constructing her response to the man called Caleb Glick, all the while wondering if it was possible to fall in love through letters. And if so, what would happen if he didn't like the way she looked?

"Dear Mr. Glick, I am writing in response to the letter that I recently received from you. I hope …" she began.

From there, Lydia talked briefly about her past and the move to her aunt's house. She definitely didn't mention that it was all for the sake of her finding a man. That was a story best left for another day, if and when they ever met in person.

After she sealed the envelope, she wondered if she sounded desperate. She *was* desperate, and besides, she did want to make it sound like she *was* interested in him.

Lydia leaned back in her chair and shook her head. Her letter made her seem so much more appealing than she really was, but she figured that was the main point of letters like that anyway—to present her best self.

She didn't expect much—if anything—to come from her response, but if something did, Lydia hoped that it would be based on truth. She wanted a man to fall in love with her for the woman she was, and not for the woman that he wanted her to be—like the man who'd wanted a replacement for his deceased wife.

Such a thing was probably unlikely or impossible, but this seemed like her last chance. With hope and an optimistic outlook, she left the letter on her desk as she climbed back into bed. Moments later, sleep came and temporarily washed away her fears and reservations.

CHAPTER SEVEN

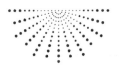

After giving the responses to her aunt in the morning, Aunt Stella assured her she'd send the letters on. Lydia carried on normally, not really expecting to ever hear back. She'd told Caleb she would be interested in writing to him, but to the others, she'd told them that she wasn't ready for commitment. She didn't know a polite and honest way to let them down gently and the last thing she wanted to do was to hurt anyone's feelings. She had written to Caleb Glick in faith to show God that she was adding works to faith. Besides that, her aunt had put herself out for her and she had to match that effort her aunt was giving.

After days, no reply had come and Lydia was feeling depressed. She'd been to a Sunday meeting and had met all the men from the community, and there was no one who suited her.

One particular Tuesday, things brightened up. When Lydia arrived back home from fetching some groceries, she walked into the house to find her aunt waiting for her in the living room with a letter gripped tightly in her hands.

"He wrote back! One of the men wrote back," she said, leaping to her feet. "Here, see what he said."

Lydia was taken aback by her aunt having opened her letter, but she knew Stella had only the best intentions. "Let me see!" Lydia said, reaching for the swaying letter in her aunt's hand.

Aunt Stella smiled and handed it to her, waiting patiently to hear what Lydia thought about what the man had to say. "Just don't get discouraged if it's not what you wanted to hear, my dear," she said, offering her niece one more reason to be worried.

With anticipation coursing through her body, Lydia barely even worried over what her aunt had said. As she pulled the letter from the envelope, her hands trembled violently, almost causing her to fumble with it. Calming herself, she read the letter silently twice before looking up from it. She stared at her aunt in shock, handing her the letter as a faint smile found its way to her lips. "He wants to get to know me!"

Aunt Stella smiled. "It seems like it, *jah*."

"His name is Caleb, and he says that he's a farmer. I didn't know he was a widower." She hadn't written to that other widower, but perhaps she wasn't meant to know Caleb was also widowed when she read his first letter.

"Then perhaps you should send him a reply right away. He seems genuinely interested in you, and if that's the case, then you need to see this through." Aunt Stella handed the letter back to her.

"I will, I will." Lydia backed out of the room and hurried up to her bedroom. She wanted to write back while she still felt the excitement and happiness of it all. Maybe he was someone who could love her for the good and kind person she was inside.

Lydia spent over an hour on her letter, asking him various questions while revealing a lot about her own life. Other than her less than perfect appearance, she was honest about everything, so she hoped that he wouldn't hold that one omission against her too greatly.

The next morning, she posted the letter. It would be several days before his next response came in, but that day brought even greater news.

Lydia was watering the flowers in the front yard when Aunt Stella arrived back from town with the mail. She handed her a letter, another one from Caleb, and Lydia rushed off to read it in private at the kitchen table.

As she read through the letter, Lydia found herself laughing at his sense of humor and wit. For the first time in ages, she was enjoying some male attention. Even though they hadn't met, she felt like she had known him for ages. The only thing that worried her now was at some point he'd suggest that they meet. She wondered if she could lose weight fast, but even if she did, she would still be a large woman.

Their exchange of letters continued on for the next few months before the question that Lydia had been waiting for finally came. She was chopping vegetables in the kitchen when Aunt Stella came back from collecting the mail with good news. Another letter had arrived, and unable to keep her curiosity at bay, she opened it immediately and read it through.

"Oh my!" she said, staring at her aunt in surprise. "He's asked me to marry him!"

Aunt Stella looked at her, open-mouthed, and Lydia pulled out a chair so her aunt could sit down.

"That is wonderful, my dear! I told you not to give up hope," her aunt said with a wide smile. "Go on; what else does he say?"

Lydia looked back down at the letter. "Just that he looks forward to meeting me and starting a life together. I think this could really be it," she said, smiling at her aunt.

"Then what are you waiting for? Write back and tell him yes!" she said, a hint of laughter in her voice. "Your parents will be so happy."

Lydia sighed, not really caring what

anyone would think. *"Jah,* they will. I'm going to respond right now, Aunt Stella. Just as soon as I finish chopping the vegetables."

Stella laughed. "You go up to your room and write back now. I can cut these."

"Denke. I'll help with the rest when I come back."

"Okay, my dear," she said as Lydia hurried away from the kitchen.

She reread the letter again. He talked about longing to marry again, and how important love was—true love. God had found the right man for her. Only a man who believed in true love would be able to look past her flaws.

Lydia's response went out the next day, but she just couldn't wait weeks to hear back. From that moment on, life seemed to grind to a halt. Every day was spent thinking about this man, Caleb. She even found herself asking the postmaster to double check to see if a letter had arrived for her. Then, the letter she'd been waiting for finally came.

Caleb's latest letter contained his joyous reaction to her acceptance, along with enough money to make the trip to Ephrata to see him. Ephrata was close to Lydia's home community, so Lydia wouldn't live far from her parents. Lydia was elated at the prospect, even though it meant that she would be leaving the security of her aunt and her home. It was a difficult choice to make, but life would never get any better if she didn't marry, and this was probably the only chance she'd have to do just that.

CHAPTER EIGHT

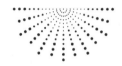

The day for her to meet Caleb had arrived. He had arranged for her to stay with a family until their wedding. Lydia hoped she'd fit in with the family. Her stomach was a violently churning pit of nerves and apprehension, but her aunt talked her through and calmed her.

Lydia stood on the platform up until the final call for the train's departure. The loud noise and the people darting about brought her back to the day when she left her parents' house. With tears filling her eyes, she turned to her aunt for one last hug.

"Everything will work out, my dear," Aunt Stella said, fighting to hold back her own tears. "Now go, before you miss your chance at happiness." Tears filled Stella's eyes. "I'll miss your laughter and your company."

Lydia swallowed hard, nodding all the while. "Goodbye, Aunt Stella, and *denke* for everything you've done for me," she said before she stepped onto the train. She quickly took her seat and then gazed out the window one last time. Waving to her aunt, she didn't stop looking at her until she was out of sight.

The hours on the train crawled by at a snail's pace, but she had high hopes for when she got to her destination. Even if Caleb was initially put off by her appearance, he seemed a nice enough man to accept her as she was. She was still concerned, but refused to let it ruin what could be the start of a new and better life.

The last several minutes seemed to go by more quickly, and Lydia was thankful for that. She arrived in Ephrata after what felt like weeks since her departure, ready to start a new life and be done with trains in general. When it pulled into the station and opened its doors, she was one of the first passengers to exit, anxious to meet her future husband.

When she stepped onto the platform, Lydia quickly scanned the faces in the crowd, hoping to find Caleb, but she wasn't able to see any Amish man. She moved further from the train, and then through the crowd she saw an Amish man walking toward her.

It was a good sign that he was smiling. She smiled back at her future husband, studying him. He was much older than she thought he would be and he was shorter than her height, though not by much she saw as he drew closer.

"Excuse me? Are you Lydia?"

"Jah, and you're Caleb?"

He nodded and then looked down as though he was embarrassed. Immediately Lydia knew what the problem was. He was making his disappointment in her appearance more than obvious.

"I have something to share with you before ... before we leave this station."

"What is it?"

He looked down at her bag and picked it up. "Let's sit over there." They made their way to a seat and sat down. "I wrote to you about true love and how important it is."

Lydia nodded, still anxious to hear the problem. If it wasn't her appearance, what could it be? "Oh, yes. I believe the same."

He stared into her eyes. "Do you?"

"I do."

"Well you'll be happy for me, then. A young lady I've liked for some time has just accepted my marriage proposal."

Frozen in place, trying to take it in, she stared at him with her mouth gaping open. "You ... you proposed to *me*."

"Before that, though, I proposed to Sally. At first she said no, but when she found out you were coming to marry me, she finally agreed to marry me."

Shaking her head, Lydia said, "How is this supposed to make me happy?"

"You said you believed in true love."

She shook her head again, scarcely believing his words. He was the most unprincipled man she'd ever come across or even heard about. "There's nothing true about it. You propose to me and someone else at the same time?"

"There's no need to be upset. I proposed to her first, before I proposed to you."

"She said no, didn't she?"

"She said no, but now she's saying yes."

The whole trip had been a waste. Lydia

shook her head. "I'll get on the next train back."

"I've arranged for you to stay at a friend's house."

"*Nee.* I'll go home. Tell them *denke,* but I will return to my aunt's."

"Why not make the most of your visit? I haven't told anyone why you're here and there are single men here. You might like one of them."

"Are they all like you?"

He smiled and nodded.

"Well, I'll go back home for certain, then." She stood and picked up her bag and made to walk off.

"Don't be like this, Lydia."

She turned around and stared at him. "You wrote me a bunch of lies and I've come here to marry you, only to find out you already asked a different woman. What am I, your backup plan?"

He stood there staring at her. And he was

a lot older than she thought he'd be, too. He must've been close to fifty. "And not only that, you weren't truthful in your letters." *You're old enough to be my vadder,* she wanted to say. And then she wanted to tell him that he wasn't the man she hoped he'd be. She wanted a man to want her and only her. He hadn't mentioned in his letters that he'd previously proposed to another woman or that another woman held a special place in his heart. If this Sally woman hadn't said yes, she would've married Caleb not knowing he had recently been in love with someone else.

Caleb's face was red now, but his eyes were still dark and lifeless. "Well, this wouldn't have worked out anyway. I'm sorry you came all this way for nothing."

It was another rejection, another disappointment. "Goodbye, Caleb."

"I can't just leave you here, are you sure—"

"Just go, Caleb."

When he turned and walked away, Lydia sat back down and leaned back on the bench, slightly embarrassed by the stares she was getting. She wasn't sure what to think or how to feel, but for some reason, she just couldn't help laughing at the ordeal. Perhaps it was her way of avoiding the fear and worry that were coming, but she could see the funny side of it all. He'd lied about being old, and she hadn't told him she was much larger than a normal woman. Each had misled the other. As she saw it from the funny side, it didn't escape her notice that the scene ended with him having a marriage partner and her still being on her own. That part had no funny side.

Sitting there by herself as the platform slowly emptied, Lydia stared off into the distance. It was much colder in Ephrata than it had been at her aunt's, and she now had nowhere to go. Other than Caleb, she didn't know anyone in the area, which made it all worse. What was she going to do now? She definitely couldn't face the train ride back, and face having to tell her aunt the embarrassing story on her return.

"Excuse me, Miss, but are you okay?" asked a deep, smooth voice.

Lydia looked up to see a tall man staring down at her. "Uh… yes, I'm fine," she said, caught in a slight daze by his unexpected appearance.

"I don't mean to pry, but I drove Caleb here and then when he came back to the car in a fluster he told me why he had asked me to drive him here."

"Oh." She looked to the ground embarrassed. "He told you he asked me to come here to marry him, and then when I get here, he tells me he is marrying someone else?"

He sat down next to her. "Yep. I told him he could make his own way home. That's no way to treat a lady, or to treat anyone."

At least she had someone on her side. She

smiled at the handsome *Englischer.* "How do you know him?"

"I used to be Amish and I lived in a neighboring community to Caleb, and I guess he asked for a ride to save the taxi fare. I'm the only person he knows with a car."

"I come from a community close by. What community did you belong to?"

"Bishop John Hostetler was—"

"That's where my parents are from."

"Really? What are their names?"

"Mike and Deborah Raber."

He smiled. "I remember them. I knew them years ago. I haven't been in the community for a long time."

It comforted her that he was from the same place.

"Are you going to be okay?" he asked.

"I don't know. I'm still trying to take it all in."

"Caleb said you'd come from Allentown. Will you go back tonight?"

"I was there staying with my aunt, but I'm not ready to go back. I just got here, but since things didn't go exactly as planned... I don't know..."

"Oh," he said, his voice filled with sympathy. "Mind if I keep you company for a while?"

"Not at all," Lydia replied, confused but delighted by his presence. "Please do."

CHAPTER NINE

"My name is Benjamin Dawson, by the way," the man said. His soft eyes and warm smile drew Lydia in almost immediately. He was a complete stranger, but for some reason he seemed to care more than everyone else did.

"Hello, Benjamin. I'm Lydia Raber," she said, smiling back. "I hope my voice wasn't raised. I don't usually yell at people at train stations," she said, hoping to make light of the incident.

"Of course not!" he replied, with a hearty

chuckle. "Well, I didn't hear what played out because I was in the car."

Lydia nodded, remembering now that he'd said he had been waiting in the car.

"Did you know Caleb before you met him today?" he asked.

Lydia sighed, looking at the ground as she thought about all that had happened. "I only knew him through his letters. His mother knows my aunt. I came to meet him and now I'm disappointed. He wasn't what I expected."

"What did you expect?"

Confused, Lydia looked up and shook her head. "What do you mean?"

Benjamin laughed. "You said that things went sour because he wasn't what you expected him to be. What were you expecting?"

Lydia squinted, unsure of what to make of his awkward question. "Not much, I suppose. All I wanted was for us to like each other and for him not to be marrying someone else when I got here."

"Is there anything I can do to make it a bit easier?"

She wasn't sure why he was being so kind. "You wouldn't happen to know of any accommodation around here, would you?" she asked. "Somewhere close by. I don't want to return to my aunt's just yet. I'd rather stay overnight here and go back tomorrow."

"Well," Benjamin said, his chin falling onto a balled fist. "There's that place over on East Main, but I don't know if they have any rooms. You could also try—"

Lydia let out a long, drawn-out sigh and covered her face with her palms. "I just need somewhere to stay until I can face the journey back home," she murmured, slowly pulling her hands away from her face.

"May I ask why you agreed to marry him? Unless that's too personal a question."

"It's a long story."

Benjamin smiled brightly, his eyes seeming even softer now. "If you're willing to share your story then I'm all ears."

Lydia swallowed nervously, her stomach aflutter all of a sudden. It would feel good to unburden her mind and get it all out. It wouldn't hurt to tell this man things about herself. He wasn't Amish anymore, so it wouldn't matter if he learned the truth about her. It wasn't as though he was a potential husband. And she'd be unlikely to ever see him again.

After she took a deep breath, she began. "It started back home with my family. I have younger sisters who are small and thin and beautiful. My parents packed me off to my aunt's house in Allentown. They hoped I'd have a better chance turning heads there, I guess. They didn't force me to go, I didn't mean it like that. I agreed it was a good idea. I'm twenty five and unmarried, so I'm an oddity."

"Join the club." Benjamin laughed and tilted his head, his eyes never leaving hers. "That does sound rather sad," he said, looking up at the sky for a moment. "But how did you end up here, meeting Caleb? Is that where your aunt comes in. She arranged all this?"

"Oh, well, to cut a long story short, yes. She urged me to write to a couple of men she'd lined up. Caleb seemed nice and we exchanged lots of letters and he eventually asked me to marry him. When I arrived, he hits me with the news that he's already marrying someone else. Someone he asked a long time ago. She said no back then, but she said yes to him just recently, apparently. So recently that he didn't have time to tell me before I got on the train. And, he expected me to be pleased for him."

"You haven't had much luck lately, have you?" he asked, standing up. Benjamin then leaned down and picked up her luggage.

"How about we find you a place to stay? It's going to get dark in a few hours, and with the dark comes the cold. I can't just leave you out in the cold. I'll walk you to a place nearby."

"Thank you," she replied as she stood. He was so kind and caring, so unlike the man she'd come there to meet. Benjamin seemed to see right past her appearance in ways that nobody had before; not even her own family.

Lydia followed him, curious to know just how far they'd be going. She walked with him through the busy station. When she turned to look up at Benjamin, he smiled. He was so tall she felt almost dainty beside him.

"I don't suppose you'd care to hear my story?" he asked while glancing over. "It's nothing like yours, but I think you'd be able to relate a bit."

"Sure, I'd love to hear it," she said, genuinely curious to know more about the mysterious man. A few more steps and they were out of the station and making their way along the busy street, with the cool wind chilling her bare neck. She pulled her coat higher and flipped up the collar to keep warm.

"I might not look old enough to be a widower, but I am, unfortunately. My wife died some years back and it broke my heart. She was funny, caring, and maybe even a little outspoken—quite like yourself." He gave a small chuckle. "Anyway; after she died, I met a wonderful woman over the Internet. She said she used to be Mennonite, and everything she said sounded so believable and convincing. The plan was we'd marry. Instead she took the money I sent her and I never heard from her again, and that's how the story ends."

"That's dreadful. You arranged to marry before you met her?"

"Yes, but we Skyped and everything, so I thought I knew her. I believed everything she said. I had no reason not to. All along she was just waiting for me to send her money, I guess."

"That is horrible," Lydia said, her chest tightening. Why would someone hurt someone so kind and considerate?

"I felt like the fool that I was. We all have our stories," Benjamin said. "But here we are," he added, pointing to a building just yards away.

Lydia looked over and saw a large sign that read, *Rooms Available.*

"Thank you for bringing me here."

"You're very welcome. I should probably leave now, but may I ask you one last question?"

"Of course," she replied.

"Would you care to meet me for dinner tonight? I can come back in about two hours or so."

"Really?"

He nodded. "If you'd like to."

"I would love to."

"We might be able to share a few more stories."

Lydia's nodded.

"Bye, Lydia. I'll see you a little later."

CHAPTER TEN

*A*fter the exchange, Lydia felt like she was floating. She watched his tall sturdy frame stride away. Then, she hurried inside with her bag and walked up to the large wooden desk that sat front and center in the lobby.

"Good afternoon," said a deep, thunderous voice. Behind the desk was a tall older man with gray eyes.

"Hello, I'm just looking for a room."

"Well, we have plenty of those, so you'll

have to be a bit more specific," he said, still focused on her with his disinterested eyes.

"Any room for a single." Lydia was annoyed at the tone of his response.

"Very well." He pulled open one of the drawers. The man shuffled around in it before lifting up a key. He then pointed to a thick pad of paper that lay on top of the desk. "Fill in your name and address, and sign here. You'll be staying in room six. It's up the stairs."

Lydia nodded and filled out the form, accepting the key. She was not looking forward to dealing with that man again while she was there, but she'd be gone in the morning. She turned away from the desk and headed toward the staircase. It wasn't long before her mind focused back on Benjamin

After climbing the stairs to her room on the second floor, Lydia hurried toward the door numbered 'six.' She quickly pushed the key in the hole and turned furiously, dropping her bag and closing the door the moment she was inside. She locked the door. Then, she ran over to the window and stared out of it. There he was, still walking off in the distance. She wished that he had just stayed with her, but then gasped at the thought. It was a relief that she would see him one last time, but now she was beginning to wonder what her emotions were really trying to tell her.

In all her years, Lydia had never felt such a connection with someone. Not only was he attractive and well spoken, he was kind, considerate, and so sweet. He spoke honestly around her, was willing to listen to her rambling, and he even laughed at the funny things she said. Those were things that happened rarely, let alone all at once. She wasn't the slightest bit embarrassed to tell him of her past, and he'd openly told her an embarrassing story of his own.

And then there was the fact that he hadn't

even mentioned her weight, or given her one of "those looks" that she'd gotten whenever she met a new man. Usually, when a man laughed around her, it was at her appearance and not for whatever witty thing she had said. With Benjamin, it was so different. It was almost as though he saw right past her rough exterior and straight into her heart. Perhaps he was just lonely and wanted the attention of anyone willing and able to give it to him.

Even if that were true, it had never happened to her before. Not once had Lydia ever been lucky enough to meet a man so desperate that he was willing to overlook her weight. If Benjamin just wanted company, then that would be fine in itself, but what if it was more than that? What if he was actually attracted to her?

"I doubt it," she mumbled, shaking her head. Lydia let out a long sigh as she headed over to the large bed in the center of the room. It felt hard when she pressed it with her hands and less than comfortable when she sat down, but it would have to suffice for a night.

As she lay back on the harsh mattress, Lydia looked up at the ceiling and wondered how the scuffmarks and smudges had landed there, so high. The room was on the road-side of the building. She closed her eyes and listened to the cars whooshing past, and every now and again she'd hear an angry horn honking.

For the first time since leaving home, she felt peaceful on the inside. Sure, dinner could go horribly wrong and make things even worse, but even the pessimistic girl that lived inside her had trouble believing that something would go wrong tonight.

The way she and Benjamin had been able to talk about anything, even the hardships of their lives, gave Lydia reason to be hopeful. They could share laughs, or be serious and honest, and do everything else that most men refused to take part in when it came to her. He was the first man that she actually enjoyed talking with; it was easy and enjoyable, so completely unlike conversing with the others.

Lydia lay there for a while, her eyes almost shutting several times over. That train ride had worn her out. If she didn't have dinner plans that night, sleep would have been all too welcome.

Instead, she rolled over and got up from the bed, and began to unpack. When she got to the bottom of the bag, she found her dress. It was the one that her Aunt Stella had helped make, and even though it hadn't helped her at dinner that first night when her aunt's invited people were over, she hoped things would go better with Benjamin. The only thing was that he had left the community.

Holding the dress up to the mirror, she smiled and nodded. Yes, that was definitely what she would wear to dinner. Lydia was so excited that she couldn't sit still any longer. Even if dinner was a couple hours off, she wanted to look perfect for him—or at least as perfect as she could get.

Never someone to waste time beautifying herself, Lydia went against the grain this *one* time. If any man had ever been worth impressing, then Benjamin was that man. She used an iron she'd found in the wardrobe to rid the dress of all its wrinkles. Then, she polished her shoes until they shone, and then she brushed through the tangles in her thick curly hair. About an hour and a lot of un-ladylike words later, she was ready; and for the first time ever, Lydia actually liked the woman who was looking back at her from in the mirror. Mirrors weren't allowed at her father's house nor at her aunt's. She'd had to be content with looking in a window reflection or using the side of a saucepan, but those reflections were often distorted.

CHAPTER ELEVEN

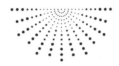

*L*ater that evening, a gentle knock sounded on Lydia's door. Hoping it was Benjamin she looked through the peephole in the door to find that it was he. She opened it to see that he wore a finely-pressed charcoal-gray suit, and his smile was brighter than ever.

"I hope it's okay that I came up to your room." He rubbed the back of his neck and looking a little sheepish. "But that clerk downstairs was kind of odd. Luckily, he gave

me your room number without much trouble, though I guess he shouldn't do that."

Lydia smiled, so happy to have met
someone like him. Not only did he have a
similar sense of humor, but more impor-
tantly, she could tell that he was trustworthy.

"I don't mind at all."

"I'm glad. I thought it might be more
memorable if we walked to the restaurant
under the moonlight. I haven't been able to
keep my feet on the ground since I met you,
so I figured it would be appropriate," he said,
laughing at himself. "We can stargaze on the
way. Stars are my favorite things to look at."
He looked at her and smiled. "One of my favorite things to look at."

Lydia chuckled at his flirting. She'd never
had anyone do that with her.

Once they were away from the building,
they walked side-by-side.

"So, you like stars, you said?"

Benjamin glanced down at her. "If I'd had

a better education, I would've made a study of the stars and found out more about our world—the earth, the stars and the solar system." He was more serious now. "That kind of thing has always intrigued me, but we don't all get to live our dreams. I can still admire God's handiwork, anyway."

As they walked down the dimly lit street, Lydia couldn't help intermittently glancing over at Benjamin, hoping to glean some hint of what he thought of her. Did he like her dress, or did he hate it? Was her hair too wavy and unkempt the way little strands found their way out the sides of her *kapp?* Maybe it was the shoes; she should have polished them just a bit longer!

"Is something wrong?" he asked, snapping her out of her mental anguish.

"Oh... no," Lydia replied, attempting to avoid eye contact until she could compose herself. "I just..."

And then Benjamin stopped, and asked

her to face him. "Please, Lydia, tell me what's on your mind."

With a loud sigh, she turned to him and shook her head. "I'm just nervous; that's all. It isn't too often a handsome man asks me to dinner." It had never happened to her, handsome man or not; no one had ever asked her out to dinner.

Benjamin stared at her sharply, his eyes quickly softening. "Well, you're entitled to feel nervous, but there's no need. And where is this handsome man you speak of?" he asked looking around.

Lydia laughed. "You can't see him, but I can."

"It's okay to be concerned," he said, his voice full of sincerity. "Words can't express how happy I am to have met you at the station today. I don't often find someone who's so easy to talk to."

Lydia could see the affection in his eyes as he spoke, but she wasn't sure just how to respond. Swallowing nervously, she stepped backward and shook her head. After a few moments of deep thought, she spoke slowly. "I don't know why you'd feel that way, but I can't say that I don't understand it. I'm glad we met today, too."

Benjamin didn't reply right away, but when he did, his awkward grin made her smile. "It took you long enough to admit it," he said, with a laugh.

It was nice to know someone so similar, yet so different from her. Still, she couldn't make sense of why he was being that way toward *her*. "It's not that; I just... look at me," she said, her eyes falling to the ground in shame.

Suddenly, his finger lifted her chin until she stared into his eyes. He said softly, "I *am* looking at you, and all I see is beauty."

"No," Lydia sighed, shaking her head. "I'm not beautiful."

"Yes, you are," he said, slowly removing

his hand. "You're beautiful on the outside, and from what I know of you so far, you're just as beautiful on the inside as well. And *that* is a very rare thing."

"How so?" she asked.

Benjamin laughed and shook his head. "For starters, you don't put up a false front like most women. You're honest; brutally even, I suspect. With you, I believe that what you see is what you get."

Lydia smiled, but it quickly faded as she looked down at herself. "And what you see *and* get is a big woman. Most men don't like that about me. Don't you think I'm rather too big?"

With a soft sigh, he reached for her hand and took it in his own. "That isn't what I see when I look at you. I see grace, beauty, and elegance. And no, I wouldn't say you're big at all, you're of a just-right size." He let go of her hand and lifted the back of his hand to her cheek. "And your skin is so soft."

Lydia swallowed excessively, her cheeks feeling impossibly hot all of a sudden. Why would someone so wonderful and perfect be so sweet to *her?* Never before had she felt this way and she'd only just met him today.

CHAPTER TWELVE

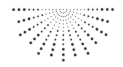

$\mathcal{A}$s they continued their walk under the moonlight, Lydia caught glimpses of people walking by. Some laughed as they covered their faces, while others just stared and said nothing. She knew what they were thinking, though. It was an uncommon thing for someone so handsome to be walking along with a woman so fat and unsightly. Being with Benjamin, their opinions meant nothing. To him, she was beautiful; and that was all that mattered.

When they arrived at the restaurant, a thin man dressed in a dark suit met them at the door. He showed them to a small, quaint corner of the large dining room. "Here are our menus," he said, handing one to each of them.

Lydia smiled and skimmed through it, her mind on anything *but* food. For the first time in a while, she didn't need it to comfort her. With Benjamin by her side, life just seemed so different, so much better.

After her indecisive mind had been made up, they ordered their meals and began talking. Topics ranged from their varied childhoods to their present days of each being a stressed, unappreciated adult. The more that Lydia learned about him, the more curious she grew about his wife. He had mentioned her several times, but not once had he really gone into any detail.

"I hope it's not rude of me to ask, but what happened to your wife?"

Benjamin paused immediately, a look of pain swarming over his face. Then, his glossy eyes met Lydia's and he sighed, shaking his head slowly.

"Oh, I'm so sorry!" she said, before he had a chance to speak.

"No; it's okay. I want you to know everything," Benjamin said, the torment apparent in his eyes. "Betsy died of rheumatic fever many years ago. It took me years to get over her being gone, but I finally pulled myself up out of that hole. I regret not having children, though."

"You do realize it's not too late, don't you?" Lydia asked, raising an eyebrow.

"Do you want children?"

Lydia laughed. "I thought everyone did."

"I'm sure there are some who have tossed the idea aside, but it's great to know you haven't." Benjamin's smile stretched from ear to ear.

Moments later, the gentleman in the suit

arrived with their meals. He balanced everything like a performer of some sort, nearly dropping her soup at one point.

After talking about anything and everything they could think of, dinner was finally reaching its conclusion. As she ate the last of her meal, Lydia looked up to see Benjamin watching her carefully with a sparkle in his eyes.

"Would it be madness if I were to ask you to marry me?" His voice was soft.

Lydia gasped as a heavy feeling sank into her stomach. At a loss, she tried to speak, but no words ever came. Instead, she swallowed hard and pursed her lips together tightly.

"You came all the way here to marry someone you had only written to a few times, right?"

Lydia nodded.

"Then why not marry me? Surely, you've learned more about me during this one dinner than you knew about Caleb in all that time."

"I suppose you're right." Her pursed lips slowly creased into a smile.

"I'm not the richest fellow in town, but I've made a comfortable home. I think you'd love it. It would be the perfect home to raise a child in, which is why all of this is just so overwhelming. I have dreams for the future; big things that I always hoped for but could never grasp. With you, I see myself reaching higher than ever before. For the last few years, I've longed for the perfect woman to share my dreams with, and in all honesty, I have yet to meet a woman better than you. I don't think one exists if I'm honest."

Lydia smiled, her chest tightening rapidly. It was still very odd to her that someone so amazing and handsome would think so highly of her. His words rang true, and since she had never felt so at ease around another human, it seemed like they were meant for each other. The two had only just met, and they were already closer than she had ever been with another person.

Just as she was about to speak, a single tear trickled down her warm cheek and heated it further. With a single little nod, she found her voice and answered, "I can't. You're not in the community."

"We're not too far apart. I do believe in God." He shook his head. "I'm sorry, it was a silly thing to ask. We don't even know each other well enough for me to ask such a thing, but can I ask you to write to me when you get back home?"

"I'd love to write to you."

"And another thing. I don't want you to think that I throw marriage proposals around. I don't. I'm a good judge of people and I like what I see. Today must've been one of the worst of your life and you handled it with grace and humility. Any other woman could quite rightly have struck Caleb."

"I could never do that." Lydia giggled and Benjamin joined in with her laughter.

"I very nearly did it on your behalf when he told me what had happened. And that was before meeting you."

"That makes me feel better, just to have someone on my side."

He took a deep breath. "We all need that."

"Would you ever return to the community?"

He stared into her eyes before he spoke. "I'm filled with doubt over a few things."

"What things? I've told you some personal things, so you can be honest with me."

"I believe in God, but why does He dole out sorrow and pain?"

"He doesn't do it."

"He allows it and sits by doing nothing to prevent it. In theory, I know all the answers and I'd spew forth these answers to others, have done so in the past, but when the tragedy struck it left me with so many unanswered questions. Real answers, that is what I'm talking about."

Lydia remained quiet. She had no answers to give him, and neither did she know how he felt because she'd never had true tragedy strike her life. Her unmarried status couldn't be compared to a life-changing event such as losing one's spouse.

"I wish I could offer you some words of comfort. Whenever I have had questions in the past I've been told we have to accept things by faith. My *vadder* says we can't explain or understand the spiritual with our carnal minds."

"I guess that's true enough. My faith ran out, until today."

When he smiled, she knew he meant when he met her. "I'm glad my visit here has done some good."

"It has."

"I'm glad you came into the train station. I don't know what I would've done if you hadn't come along. Probably I would be in my room feeling sorry for myself, but instead ..."

"Instead?" He leaned forward, smiling wider.

"Instead I'm having a great time."

"That's good to hear."

Lydia was amazed how well the conversation flowed, and that she could tell him things without feeling embarrassed or self-conscious.

"I suppose I should walk you back to your hotel, but we must exchange addresses and phone numbers first."

"Okay."

They walked back in the moonlight. It was the most romantic night Lydia could imagine. Miracles did happen, and she knew that now. She hadn't even known this man yesterday and now she knew her life had been changed.

When they got back to the small hotel, he stood on the steps.

"Thank you for coming to my rescue, Benjamin."

"I've enjoyed every minute of it. Write to me as soon as you get on the train. Don't lose my address."

She giggled. "Don't lose mine."

He patted his shirt pocket. "I've got it right here. Close to my heart. Before you go, Lydia, I need to tell you something that you should know before you decide to write." He took a step closer and his voice lowered. "I'm undecided as far as whether I'd ever return to the community and I don't want to pull you away."

"Oh, I see. Thank you for being so honest." Lydia wanted someone in the community and had never thought she'd consider someone who wasn't. Not being experienced in love, she had to wonder at Benjamin's motivation. He had certainly proposed very quickly, but that could've been a light-hearted joke or a flirtation.

"I should've mentioned it first, but then it would've been awkward if I'd mentioned such a thing too soon. We get along so well, I'm hoping I might see you again and didn't want you to leave without knowing where my head's at."

"And that's how it should be. I'm glad you told me. I don't want any more surprises like the one earlier today. Goodnight, Benjamin."

"Goodnight, Lydia. Sleep well."

She turned and walked up the steps. When she got into her room, she realized she was no longer upset by what Caleb had done to her. What Benjamin had just told her was something to make her consider whether she'd write to him, though. Her heart told her she'd met a man she'd like to marry, but her head told her there was a chance he wanted someone to take the place of his late wife. And there was the fact that he wasn't in the Amish community.

When she slid between the sheets, she decided she was happy about writing to Benjamin. Who knew what the future might hold for the two of them? Surely they'd met for a reason. It would be a cruel thing to finally meet a man she felt so at ease with, and so instantly, and then for nothing to come of it. Just as she was fading into sleep while imagining Benjamin's arms around her, the phone beside her bed beeped, causing her to jump half out of her skin. She'd barely been conscious that there was a telephone in her room. With her heart racing, she fumbled across the bedside table and picked up the phone's receiver without a thought as to who might be on the other end of the line.

"Hello?"

"I'm not calling too late, am I?

"No, not at all." She sank back into the

pillow, pleased to hear Benjamin's deep voice.

"Have you bought your ticket for tomorrow?"

"No. I was going to do that as soon as I got to the station. I don't even know the timetable. I'll just wait at the station for the next train, I guess."

"Spend the day with me, and then I'll have you to your aunt's by nightfall."

"Really?"

"Yeah. It's only an hour or so by car."

"Is that all? It feels so much longer by train, somehow."

"What do you say? Before you answer, I'll give you two choices. One, I'll drive you directly back tomorrow with no strings attached. Or, two, spend the day with me and I'll have you back to your aunt's house at a reasonable hour."

Lydia could scarcely keep the smile from her face.

"I'd really like to see you again, Lydia. Just please say you'll choose option two," he added with laughter in his deep voice.

"Okay, I'll choose two. As long as it's not putting you out too much."

"Not at all or I wouldn't have offered. I don't know why I didn't think of it before. It only occurred to me a few moments ago that I should've driven you back to your aunt's house. I could've done that today."

"I'm glad you didn't. It was nice having the time to get to know you."

"That's how I feel too."

Lydia gave a little giggle as warm tingles rippled through her body.

"I'll come for you at eight. Sleep tight, Lydia."

"Good night, Benjamin, and thank you." Lydia replaced the receiver and lowered herself in the bed. This—whatever it was—was really happening.

CHAPTER THIRTEEN

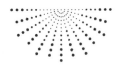

When Lydia woke the next morning, she was surprised she had been able to get at least some sleep. A smile immediately met her lips when she thought of Benjamin and spending the day with him. Glancing at the digital clock on the small table beside the bed told her it was six thirty, still early. There was plenty of time to get ready. After she had showered, she changed into the clothes she was wearing for the day. Her choice was a dark green dress and her usual cape and *kapp*.

There was nothing special about this dress, not like the one she'd worn the previous evening that had been made by Aunt Stella. When she got back she'd ask her aunt to help her sew a couple more new dresses before she went back home, since her mother had made that stupid rule about her losing weight before she sewed any more clothes. It didn't seem likely that *Mamm* would bend, and nothing made her feel worse than wearing clothes that were uncomfortably tight. When she felt bad, she tended to eat for comfort, so *Mamm's* strategy had the opposite of the desired effect.

After she had adjusted her dress, she studied herself in the mirror. She looked like any other plain woman, but she was sure Benjamin saw beyond that. Then her thoughts turned to breakfast. If he was collecting her before eight, he might have already had his breakfast. She opened the small fridge that she'd previously discovered concealed behind large double-cupboard doors.

On top of the fridge was an electric teakettle, and next to it was a basket containing an assortment of teas, sachets of coffee, and two small boxes of cereal. She opened the fridge hoping to find milk; if there was some, milk and cereal would be on her menu for breakfast. To her delight, there was a small container of milk and another of orange juice.

This place wasn't so bad after all. There were even two slices of bread wrapped in plastic and two small pats of butter. She'd have cereal first and then make herself some toast.

After she had poured the cereal and milk in a bowl, she stirred it lightly with the only spoon in the room, a teaspoon, and took the bowl over to the window. Even at that hour of the morning, the town was awake and busy.

The first thing she had noticed about Benjamin was his height and his size. Physically he was her perfect match. She'd always held the hope in the back of her mind that her husband would be a big man. She quickly pushed those thoughts out of her mind. She was getting way too far ahead of herself.

If she started thinking like that, she would get her hopes up. Besides that, she didn't even know him properly. The huge downside to it all was that he'd left the community. He had left years ago and never returned. He'd said he'd stayed away because of his wife, but she'd been gone for some years and he'd made no effort to return.

As she sat there munching on the cereal and looking out the window, she wondered what his life had been like. As far as he told her, he'd left on rumspringa fully intending to go back, and then he met a woman who had no interest in Amish life. He had allowed that woman to pull him away from God. Did that mean he was a weak man?

Lydia didn't know whether it was a good trait for him to have been so in love with the woman that he stayed out of the community. He had shown love and devotion to his wife, and true commitment. On the other hand, where was his commitment to God? Should he have given up the love of his life to return to the community without her? Or at least returned after her death?

As she spooned another teaspoonful of cereal into her mouth, she wondered what she would've wanted her ideal man to do in a situation like that. It was a romantic and lovely notion that the man gave up all to be with the woman he loved, even risking his very soul and eternity without God. Did she want a man who would turn his back on the woman he loved and return to the community alone? She wanted a man who was devoted to her, but she also wanted a man who put God first in his life. She had some heavy thinking to do.

Maybe it was a mistake meeting this man today. Again, she reminded herself that Benjamin's wife had died a long time ago and he had made no attempt to go back to the community, so that had to tell her something. Another spoonful of cereal went into her mouth.

What was she doing, about to spend the day with an *Englischer?* Because that's what he was — an *Englischer.* She was flattered by his attention and drawn in by his good looks and his manly charm. Now she could see how easy it would be for someone to be pulled away from God because of love. Especially someone in her situation, having been rejected so many times.

She glanced at the clock. If she left now, she could be back at Aunt Stella's place at lunchtime... provided she didn't have to wait long for a train. No, she couldn't do that. This man stood up for her at the very lowest point in her life. She couldn't let fear cause her to run from him, but was she walking a fine line and risking inching off the narrow path by spending time with him?

He had even taken the day off to spend with her. The least she could do is not run out on him. That would make her look as unprincipled as Caleb. Benjamin was a real man. A good man.

She knew her father and mother would be horrified if they knew she'd agreed to spend the day with a man who wasn't Amish. And since he'd left the community years ago, she didn't know if that would make her parents feel better about it or worse.

This would never be allowed to happen if she was staying at her father's house or with Stella. Aunt Stella would give her a lecture and tell her it couldn't happen. *Dat* would skip the lecture, and just forbid it.

Even though she was twenty-five, she often felt like a child, thanks to the way her parents treated her. Now that she'd had this time alone, she realized she had to make her own decisions and become more independent. That meant only one thing; she had to get a job like her sisters had done. She knew she would have to put her fears and lack of confidence aside and find a job somewhere if she was ever going to feel like an adult.

With her cereal now gone, she rinsed out the bowl in the sink and then popped the two pieces of bread into the toaster. While it was toasting, she got the butter out and ready to spread. A quick look in the fridge confirmed that there was no jam or anything else to put on the toast. She would just have to eat buttered toast like she often had at home. The butter from home would taste better, though, than these two tiny packages that looked like some form of processed butter, most likely full of chemicals and preservatives. Better to not think about that!

While she waited for the toast, she looked out the window excited for the day ahead and wanting nothing more than to see Benjamin's smiling face again.

At that moment, she decided to push her reservations aside and fully enjoy this one day with Benjamin. Something deep inside told her that he would become the yardstick to measure other men by. He would be a hard act to follow, and she hoped she wouldn't have to lower her standards when she married. No, she would not. She would only marry someone she could converse with easily, just like Benjamin, and someone with whom she felt just as comfortable. If *Gott* could bring Benjamin to rescue her after Caleb's betrayal, He could also bring the right man for her to marry.

When she'd finished breakfast and

packed all her belongings, she headed downstairs to pay for her stay. She was relieved to see a different clerk at the desk, a nice middle-aged lady. Once her bill was settled, she headed outside to wait for Benjamin.

It was a little before eight when she sat down on a seat outside the hotel. Right at eight, a car pulled up in front of her. She looked hard to see if it was Benjamin driving, and then the car door opened. Benjamin got out and hurried over to her.

"Good morning, Lydia."

She stood up and smiled. "Hello. You're right on time."

He grabbed her bag. "Are you ready?"

"Yes."

"I'll put this in the trunk."

As they pulled away from the hotel, he glanced over at her. "Thank you for spending the day with me."

"You didn't give me much time to think about it."

"If I had, you'd have found some excuse not to come with me today."

Lydia smiled at him. "Well, I thought of a few of those when I got off the phone last night."

"Well," he said, copying her with a teasing voice, "put all that out of your head. We'll have a good day. Have you had breakfast?"

"Yes, a little. What they had in my room."

"There are two farmers markets in this town and one has a wonderful café that makes the best coffee and bacon and eggs. From there, we'll decide how to spend the day. How does that sound?" He took his eyes off the road for an instant while he gave her a sideways glance.

"That sounds perfect."

CHAPTER FOURTEEN

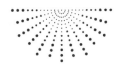

*T*hey had a wonderful day together, and Lydia liked him more every minute. Now their day was coming to an end, as they were only minutes from Aunt Stella's house. Benjamin had showed her most of the main tourist sites from Ephrata to Allentown. They'd both talked freely, and Lydia told him much more about herself and her family and listened while she learned about his life. The more they talked the more she knew she was going to miss him. Hopefully they would meet again when she went back home to her parents' house since they didn't live that far apart.

"I've had a delightful day, thank you, Lydia."

"Me too, and thank you. I don't know what I would've done if you hadn't come along yesterday." The memories of Caleb's rejection of her still hurt, but it didn't seem to matter too much now.

"You're very welcome. But I don't know what to do now. Shall I take you right up to the house, or leave you at the end of the driveway? I'm guessing your Aunt Stella won't be too happy to see you pull up in a car with a strange man driving."

"I'll tell her how you drove me here, but as you say, it's possibly better you leave me a little distance from the house and I'll walk the rest of the way."

"Okay."

"Thanks again, Benjamin. You've been very kind."

"I've loved every minute of it. Don't lose my phone number. I want to see you as soon as you get home."

"Okay." She looked away from him. She might have a hard decision to make.

"I'm not trying to lead you astray or anything."

"I know that."

"Just agree to see me once, and then I'll sort myself out. I've got a lot of thinking to do."

She smiled as she looked at him, believing his words. "Okay, I can agree to that." Had meeting her been the prompting he needed to return to *Gott?* She certainly hoped so.

Seeing her aunt's house in the distance, she said, "Here will do."

He moved the car to the side of the road and came to a halt. Then he got her bag out of the trunk.

"Here you go. Will you be alright with it?"

"I don't have far to go."

They looked into each other's eyes and Lydia hoped that he might kiss her. He took a step forward, leaned down and kissed her gently on her cheek. It wasn't the kiss she'd hoped for, but it didn't stop her heart from thumping hard.

"Bye, Benjamin."

"I'll hear from you soon, I hope. Bye, Lydia."

Lydia walked away, feeling him staring at her. A little further along, she heard his car door open and close, and the engine start up again; then she listened as the car did a U turn and headed back. Desperately she wanted to turn and look at him, but she didn't. Instead, she trudged ahead with her bag growing increasingly heavier.

Lydia hated the thought of having to tell her aunt how the man, Caleb, had rejected her right in the middle of the train station. She still couldn't get over the fact that the man expected her to be happy for him because he found true love, right as he stomped all over her broken heart. If she had been a more Godly woman she might've found a piece of happiness for him, but obviously her empathy needed working on or something.

Perhaps Benjamin only seemed good at the time because she'd been so distraught over what Caleb had done to her. But still, she was grateful that he'd come to her rescue. With him, she'd had a proper date and some innocent flirtation, which made her feel good about herself. Perhaps she'd have a better perspective on things now that she was back to Aunt Stella's house and could talk things over with her.

When she was just yards from the house, Aunt Stella opened the door and hurried toward her.

"What happened?" Stella asked, looking pale and deathly worried.

"I've got so much to tell you, Aunt Stella. Things just went horribly wrong."

Her aunt stepped in toward her and grabbed her arm. "Come inside now and tell me all about it. I've got a nice pot of soup warming on the stove. I must've known you were coming somehow."

"A hot meal sounds so good right now. And is there fresh bread?"

"I just baked some this morning."

"Good," Lydia said as they stepped through the door.

"Now you just sit down at the kitchen table; leave your things right there and come into the kitchen and tell me everything that happened."

Lydia sat down at the table, took a deep breath, and began. "As soon as I saw him I was surprised. He was a lot older than what I thought he would be, or I should say, than he'd led me to believe."

Stella jumped up and adjusted the heat of the stove and then she sat back down opposite. "I'm sorry. Go on, and then what happened?"

"He told me that he was getting married to somebody else."

"Nee!" Stella recoiled as if she couldn't believe her ears.

"I can tell you I was shocked and I didn't think I'd heard right. I'd come all that way and we had written to each other so many times. And, Aunt Stella, he expected me to be pleased for him. He said he asked this woman a long time ago and she said no, but when she found out that I was coming to marry him, she finally agreed to marry him."

Aunt Stella shook her head. "I can always see two sides of a situation. From his point of view he'd asked two women to marry him. Even though the first one said no, could he have felt obliged to her because he had asked her first?"

This was not the time for Stella to sympathize with Caleb and see his point of view. "I don't think so, Aunt Stella, because she said no. So, when she said no, his proposal was then off the table."

"*Jah,* you're right. Quite right. And that left him free to ask somebody else, and he asked you."

"Exactly. I go there expecting to marry someone, and I thought the only problem would be that he wouldn't like my size."

Stella leaned forward. "Was he a short man?"

"No, not really, just a little bit shorter than my height, but he was old. I knew from his letters how tall he was because that was one thing I asked him. I didn't tell him I was a big girl, I told him I was tall." Lydia sighed as the feelings rushed back. "It was just horrible."

"He said he'd take me to the family he'd arranged for me to stay with, and I said no, that I was going to return home."

"And then what happened, because you been gone for days?"

"It hasn't been days. I just stayed one night. I was sitting down on a bench at the station, not wanting to come home just yet because I was too upset. So I decided to stay overnight."

"That's very sensible. Traveling makes one quite weary."

"And so does being rejected. Anyway, I got talking to a nice man. He used to be Amish and he'd driven Caleb there. When Caleb got back to the car after dumping me, Caleb told Benjamin the real reason why he'd come to the train station. Benjamin was upset with him and told him to find his own way home. Benjamin found me and he calmed me down. Then he walked me to a place where I could stay the night. And then we had dinner together and the next day I came home. Here I am."

"Our God works in mysterious ways."

"You don't see it being a problem that he's an *Englischer?* He used to be Amish."

"Ah, you like him?"

"I do."

"Perhaps *Gott's* using you as bait for him to return."

Lydia laughed at her aunt's analogy. At least her aunt wasn't instantly horrified by the notion of her liking a man who wasn't in the community.

Aunt Stella leaned forward. "What's he like?"

"He's got such a lovely kind face. Eyes that can speak without any help from his mouth. And he's very tall, and he's got broad shoulders. He makes me feel dainty if that's possible."

"And how did you leave things?"

"We're going to write to one another."

"Meeting someone first before you write is probably a good thing."

Lydia nodded. "*Jah,* I found that out."

"What else do you know about him?"

"He's a widower, and that was one thing I

didn't want, a widower. He met his wife on *rumspringa.* He said he was going to go back but he couldn't leave her and she didn't want to change how she was."

Stella frowned. "You told me Caleb was a widower."

Lydia nodded. "Yes, he was, as I learned from his second letter, and that wasn't ideal, but I wrote to him all the same. Anyway, if Benjamin can overlook my size, I guess I can overlook his circumstances."

"People can't help their circumstances, but they can help leaving the community if that's what you mean." Stella stood up to stir the soup when it bubbled.

She'd hoped Aunt Stella wouldn't take such a stern view of Benjamin's leaving the community, but she did respect Stella as a voice of reason. Lydia could smell the soup now that it had heated. It was chicken and vegetable soup, something that her aunt always had on standby.

When they both had a bowl of soup and warm bread in front of them, they closed their eyes and said a silent prayer.

When Aunt Stella opened her eyes, she broke off some bread and buttered it.

"What are you thinking?" asked Lydia.

"I'm not thinking about Benjamin, I'm going to write to Caleb's mother tonight and tell her exactly what I think."

"*Nee,* don't, please. It's okay. What's done is done. Besides I'm happy that I'm not marrying him now if he's a man who's so fickle. I want a man who has a steadfast mind and knows what he wants."

"Okay, my dear. I'll keep trying to find you one and you keep writing to Benjamin to find out if he's such a man. He might return to *Gott,* you never know. Just be careful. I'll send off some more letters tomorrow."

"I don't ... I can't go through that again, Aunt Stella."

Aunt Stella leaned over and patted her

hand. "I'll select them better, just leave it up to me."

CHAPTER FIFTEEN

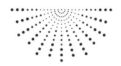

*L*ydia knew Aunt Stella was right to be wary of Benjamin. He'd been out of the community for so long, and she knew she'd never leave, and it probably wasn't realistic to believe that Benjamin would come back. It was a huge coincidence, though, that he had come from the very same community as her family.

Lydia lay back on her bed and closed her eyes, casting her mind back many years to when she was a girl. She didn't take notice of the young teenagers back then. Perhaps her mother and father would remember him.

One thing she knew was that it was exhausting looking for a husband. If Benjamin had stayed in the Amish community, she'd be feeling very differently right now.

She would keep her word, and she would write to Benjamin tomorrow. She wasn't going to give up on finding out why everything seemed so easy with him.

After breakfast, she helped Aunt Stella with chores, and by midmorning, they were both having a rest when Lydia got out pen and paper and began her letter writing.

With a cup of tea in her hand, Aunt Stella tipped her head to one side. "Are you writing to that young man you met at the station?"

"*Jah.* And I might call *Mamm* and *Dat* later today and see if they remember him."

"Wouldn't his family still be about?"

"His parents both passed away a couple of years ago, and they had stopped going to the community meetings just after he left on *rumspringa.*"

"That wouldn't encourage him to return to the community, now would it?"

"I suppose not, but it was on *rumspringa* when he fell in love."

"He could have just as easy fallen in love with someone from the community."

"I suppose so, but it just didn't happen for him."

Aunt Stella made tsk tsk sounds at the back of her throat and then took another sip of tea.

"Was he supposed to turn his back on the woman he loved?" Lydia asked.

"If he wanted his reward in heaven, then *jah.*"

"It would've been easier said than done. I mean, it wouldn't have been an easy thing to do, to be in love with someone and then just leave her."

"Very often the right thing to do is the

hardest thing."

Lydia smoothed down the sheet of paper she was just about to write on. It was hard to have a conversation with her aunt because she always saw things in black-and-white. She could only imagine how her father felt growing up and having her as his older sister. But her soft side was lovely and that's why Lydia had enjoyed her stay with Stella.

With pen poised above the paper, she asked, "Have you ever been in love, Aunt Stella?"

"*Nee,* I can't say that I have. I liked a couple of men when I was much younger, but no men suited me. Things were different back then. The communities weren't as large and that's why you should take every opportunity that is offered you. Now everyone's got a phone in their barn or in a shanty outside their house, so communication between two people is a lot easier."

"And I guess the Postal Service is quicker too."

Aunt Stella grunted and gave a nod.

Lydia put the pen on the paper and started writing. She told Benjamin she was back at Aunt Stella's house and was planning to stay there a couple of weeks longer and then she would go back home. She hoped that Benjamin would again suggest that they meet when she got back, but she knew her parents wouldn't like that. He was an *Englischer,* and ten years older, and a widower. That was not what her parents had in mind.

"I can't blame you for following your heart, but don't let any of your decisions pull you away from *Gott.* He has to come first in your life."

"Jah, always."

"I hope you don't mind me saying so."

"I don't. I'm grateful for your guidance. You're a very wise woman."

Aunt Stella gave a little chuckle. "I'll get

on with my letters too. We'll find you a man who's just right."

"I appreciate that."

She continued her letter. Even though she thought they'd talked about every possible thing the other night and during the day yesterday, she still found plenty to write about. The first question she asked him was about his family and precisely where they had lived, and she gave him her address at home to see if he had lived close by before he left the community.

LYDIA HEADED out to Stella's barn where she had the phone. She pulled open one of the two rough wooden barn doors and stepped inside and smelled the hay that was stored for Stella's two buggy horses. To the left was the buggy and she made her way across the straw-strewn floor to the far right of the barn, past the feed buckets and bags of feed. It was dark in the barn, with the only light coming in through an opening high on one wall and through the door she'd just opened.

She reached out to pick up the receiver but had to dust a cobweb away before she touched it. It was clear that Aunt Stella pre-ferred writing to people rather than tele-phoning. She dialed the number of her home and hoped that somebody would hear it ringing from the barn. After waiting until it rang itself out, she then dialed again. On the second call, Sarah answered.

"Hello."

"Sarah, it's me."

"Who?"

"Me—Lydia." Lydia rolled her eyes at her sister not recognizing her voice.

"Are you coming home soon?"

"I think so, not just now, but soon. Is *Mamm* or *Dat* there?" She looked nervously around the gloomy barn. It was scary being there alone.

"*Jah.* They're in the house."

"Can I speak to one of them?" Lydia asked growing increasingly annoyed.

"What about?"

"Just put one of them on would you?"

"Depends on what it's about."

Lydia heaved a sigh. Sarah was the type of girl who wanted to negotiate everything. In short, she was really annoying. "Put one of them on or I'll tell them when I get back that you wouldn't let me speak to them."

"I'm not stopping you from talking to them. I just want to know a bit of a hint of what it's about. I like to know what's going on, that's all."

What was the use? Lydia sighed. "If you must know, I want to ask them if they know a man who used to be in the community years ago."

"Who?"

"Just a man I met. He's not Amish anymore."

"You've got a boyfriend and he's not in the community?"

"No, that's not what I said. I want to ask them about a man who used to be in the community." She heard the phone click and then shuffling sounds, and hoped Sarah was getting one of her parents.

Holding patiently onto the receiver, she was pleased when, a few minutes later, her breathless mother answered the phone.

"Lydia, you've got a boyfriend?"

"Oh that Sarah. I'm going to wring her neck when I see her again."

"Lydia, don't let your aunt hear you say such a thing. She'll think we raised you poorly."

"No, she won't. I'm getting on great with Aunt Stella. We're so much alike. Anyway I don't have a boyfriend. I just told Sarah I wanted to ask you if you knew a man who used to be in the community. His name is Benjamin Dawson. He said he knows you and *Dat.*"

"*Jah,* I know him. He went *on rumspringa* when he was a teenager and never returned. That brings back memories. It was a long time ago."

"What was he like?"

"He seemed nice. Everybody liked him, and his parents were lovely. Although the parents left off going to community meetings around that same time."

Happiness washed away any mean thoughts she had about her younger sister.

"Did you meet him somewhere?" her mother asked.

"*Jah,* it's a long story, and I'll tell you when I get home."

"How is he?"

"He's good, very good."

"And you're having fun with Stella?"

"*Jah,* I am. She's so sweet and kind. I hope I'm like that when I'm her age. She never married either."

"You say that like you'll never get married, but you will. I've been praying that you meet a lovely man, and so is your *vadder.*"

"*Denke, Mamm.* Stella is doing everything she can to help me."

"That's good. When you come back, you should ask her if she wants to come back and stay with us for a while."

"*Jah,* that'd be good. You better get back inside the house and stop Sarah from telling everybody I've got a boyfriend."

Her mother laughed. "*Jah,* I'll put a stop to that business right away."

Lydia giggled, now able to see the funny side. "I'll call you a day or two before I come home, *Mamm.*"

"Okay. Bye now."

Lydia walked out of the barn, pleased that

her mother remembered Benjamin having been nice and also his parents.

THURSDAY CAME, and that was the night she'd agreed to go to the pizza night with a few of the single people from the community.

CHAPTER SIXTEEN

When her aunt opened the door, the wind rushed through the house. Albie and John were turning the buggy around.

Lydia turned to her aunt to say goodbye.

Aunt Stella whispered, "Enjoy yourself, my dear. I know you're nervous and parties like this aren't what you're used to, but your future is at stake. Meet and mingle, and show those men just how special you are. Hurry along now," she said, pointing to the waiting buggy.

"Goodbye. I'll be home when it's ended," Lydia said, going down the steps slowly, careful not to trip. Before she climbed up into the buggy, she looked back one more time and waved. She climbed into the buggy and greeted the two men who'd been so kind as to invite her.

When they arrived at the restaurant, Lydia was ushered in with the other guests. John and Albie introduced her to the others. It was too loud and seemed overly cheerful, and even though she was amongst Amish, for some reason she still felt completely out of place. There were ten of them, all sitting around a large table talking. They were polite and tried to engage her in conversation, being careful not to leave her out. She was grateful for that. When nerves got the better of her, she excused herself and walked to the ladies' room.

She had to pass a table where two handsome well-dressed men were sitting with two women. One of the men looked at her and said something to the other. Then one of the ladies at their table glanced at her and cackled.

One of the men leaned over and said, "The buffet's that way."

Lydia could feel the blood draining from her face. She felt cold and ugly, hated and ridiculed. The only thing she could do was ignore them and keep walking while hearing them sniggering behind her.

Once in the bathroom, she splashed her face with cold water and did her best to pull herself together. Albie and John had been nice enough to invite her to their singles' night. She would ignore the rude people; she didn't know them anyway, and she would show respect to the Amish people she was with—Albie, John, and their friends.

She walked back past the same people and was glad they didn't say another word to her. Then she did her best to be friendly with the young people at the table. To her surprise the rest of the night was enjoyable even though there was no one there she would consider as a potential husband.

THE NEXT DAY just after the midday meal, Lydia was having a quiet moment and thinking about Benjamin. She was still upset about those horrible people teasing her last night. It just wasn't fair. Everyone thought she was big from overeating but she watched what other people ate, and she ate about the same. She thought her aunt might be right about doing exercise. And then she decided to get off the bed and go for a walk; it couldn't hurt to go for a walk out in the fresh air. Maybe that would kick-start her body shedding some extra pounds. Surely that would help her a bit. As she walked downstairs, she saw Aunt Stella at the bottom staring up at her.

"There you are, dear. I was just coming up to get you."

Lydia could see a letter in her aunt's hand. She couldn't stop the smile that she knew was spreading across her face. "Is that from Benjamin?"

"I didn't mean to snoop but in the back of it, it did say it was from Benjamin."

Lydia ran down the rest of the stairs, plucked the envelope from Aunt Stella's hands while saying a quick thank you, and hurried over to the couch. She ripped open the letter to see what he had to say. When she had finished speed-reading the letter, she read it again, this time more carefully. He said he would easily be able to stay in the same job as landscape gardener if he returned to the community. Lydia giggled when she read that bit about what he did for a living. They had talked about so many things, but she didn't even think to ask him what he did for a living. That could explain why he was so well muscled, carrying all that soil, and heavy plants, and such.

He asked her to let him know when she went back home. Did that mean that he wanted her to visit him? Yes, she told herself, of course that's what he meant. She could see herself married to this man, and it didn't sound like he wanted her to fill the role his late wife had held. It sounded like he truly liked *her*. She placed the letter in her lap and she couldn't help smiling.

"Good news?" Aunt Stella asked.

She looked over at her aunt who was just coming out of the kitchen. "It sounds like he's thinking seriously of coming back to the community."

"That is good news." Aunt Stella hurried over and sat opposite with her hands in her lap and looking expectantly at Lydia.

Her aunt was sitting there waiting to hear

what he said in his letter. Lydia kept the parts to herself about him saying how much he enjoyed their dinner together and told her the more general things in his letter.

"Of course, I can't say I want him to come back for me. The decision has to be his, and his alone."

Aunt Stella nodded. "True, very true. Are you going to write back to him?"

"I'll write back to him tonight, and I'll go into town and post it tomorrow."

"Excellent."

"I'll put this letter up in my room, and then I will go for a walk."

"It sounds like a great idea, and if I wasn't so old, I might come with you." Aunt Stella chuckled.

WALKING ALONG NEXT to the barbed-wire fence that separated Aunt Stella's house from the neighboring property, Lydia turned her face up to the warm afternoon sun and allowed the calming rays to filter through her body. It was peaceful at Stella's place, but she missed her mother and the rest of her family. Maybe it was time to go home. She walked further to the end of the driveway where it met the road and walked along the side of it a little way. The dirt road rarely saw traffic, as Stella lived well away from any main roads.

The further she walked the more overgrown the sides of the roads were with long weeds and the occasional clump of wildflowers. She was forced to walk on the road's edge. When she became aware that she was sweating, she turned around and headed back.

The walk in the fresh air and the sun had helped to clear her mind. She would go home and do her best to persuade Aunt Stella to go with her.

After she showered and put on a clean

dress, she found her aunt in the sewing room. She leaned against the wall and said, "I'm thinking of going home soon."

Stella took her foot off the treadle and looked at her. "So soon?"

"Jah, why don't you come and stay awhile? *Dat* and *Mamm* would love to have you visit."

"Nee, I've got too many things going on. Next week I've got a fundraiser, and then there's all these other things."

"When would you be able to visit?"

"I don't know. I hoped you would've been able to stay longer."

"I feel I should go. But I've enjoyed the stay here."

Aunt Stella smiled. "I've liked having you. I might make it for Christmastime."

"That would be lovely."

"Well, figure out when you want to go."

"Maybe the day after tomorrow."

"Okay." Aunt Stella looked back at her sewing.

"I'll put the dinner on." Lydia hurried out of the room, pleased to be going back home. Her stay with her aunt had served its purpose, but not at all as expected.

CHAPTER SEVENTEEN

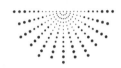

Two days later, Lydia got out of the taxi and headed toward the door of her family's house, holding her bag. The door opened, and her sisters came running out of the house squealing.

"Lydia! You didn't even tell us you were coming home," Paula called out as she ran to her.

"What's happening? Did you meet a man? Can I have your room?" The words tumbled out of Sarah's mouth one after the other.

Lydia giggled. "Not just yet. That's the answer to the last of your questions."

"That sounds hopeful," Paula said.

"I've got a few things I can tell you girls tonight about my stay with Aunt Stella." She leaned closer and spoke more quietly.

Paula took her bag from her. "I'll put this upstairs, and you go see *Mamm* in the kitchen. She's just got her hands into some batter and couldn't come out."

When Lydia got to the kitchen, her mother was washing her hands in the kitchen sink, and she turned around and smiled at her.

"It's so good to see you home. We've all missed you." Her mother gave her a hug.

"I've missed everyone too. Where's *Dat?*"

"He'll be along soon. He's just helping someone repair their barn. Now sit down and tell me everything that happened."

Sarah was the first to sit down and she

fixed her eyes upon Lydia as she and her mother sat down at the table.

"Well, there's quite a lot to tell. Aunt Stella did her best to match me with someone in her community, but there were only really two men my age there."

Her mother leaned back. "Only two?" she asked with raised eyebrows.

"Jah."

"I would've thought there would be a lot more than that with the way she was talking."

"Me too, but there wasn't anyone else. Anyway, neither of them suited me even though they were very nice."

""What was wrong with them?" asked Sarah.

"Nothing, they just didn't suit me."

Paula came into the kitchen and sat down with them.

"There's so much to tell."

Their mother said, "I knew there would

be a lot more because you've been away for so many weeks."

"It was months," Paula added, her eyes on Lydia, too.

"I had the option of writing to a few men that Stella found for me. They were sons of some of her many friends. I chose one man that I liked, based on his letter, and we wrote back and forth quite a few letters. And then he proposed."

Sarah's eyes grew wide while their mother gasped.

"Without you meeting him?" Paula asked.

"Jah, he lives in Ephrata."

"That's so close," the mother said. "When do we meet him?"

"Why didn't you tell us?" Sarah asked.

"I didn't want to say anything until I met him. And then I went on the train to meet him—"

"So are you getting married or what?" asked Sarah frowning.

"Nee, because when I got off the train, he met me and said that he'd asked a girl to marry him months ago, and she said no, but then when she heard I was coming she changed her mind and said yes."

"So you are *not* marrying him?" asked Sarah.

"Nee. That's what he told me when I arrived there. He was going to marry the other girl, not me"

"That's dreadful," their mother said.

"We know people from Ephrata. What's his name?" asked Paula.

"His name is Caleb Glick."

"Nee!" Paula slapped her hand over her mouth as her eyes bugged wide.

Lydia looked at Paula and, judging by her sister's reaction, figured that she knew Caleb, or had heard of him.

"What is it?" Lydia asked.

"Winston's sister, Sally, is marrying Caleb Glick from Ephrata."

Their mother shook her head. "This is not good."

"This is dreadful, Lydia. How can someone agree to marry you and then when you go to meet them they tell you that they're marrying someone else?" Paula asked. "It's not right."

Lydia shrugged. "I know. That's just how it happened. He had arranged for me to stay with a family there until we got married and everything. And once everything was arranged I was going to let all of you know. And then all my hopes were dashed."

Paula sprang to her feet. "I'm going to give Winston's family a piece of my mind. I'm very upset about this."

"*Nee* don't. It worked out all right in the end because I didn't like him, not like that."

Paula sat down. "You must've liked him if you agreed to marry him."

"But not anymore; not with the way he treated me."

"I'm going to go over there right now," Paula said. "Sally had her chance. She should've stuck to the decision she made."

"No, don't," Lydia urged.

Paula sprang to her feet anyway, and marched out of the house.

"Stop her, *Mamm*," Lydia urged, knowing that Paula wouldn't listen to her. She might listen to their mother.

"Don't worry about her. It's probably just an excuse to see Winston again. He'll calm her down."

"Do you think so?" Lydia asked.

"Jah, I do."

"I don't want them to get in an argument over me."

"Nothing would ever come between them," Sarah said.

"I just don't want a fuss to be made. It's all worked out for the best for me." Now she knew she couldn't tell anyone about Benjamin just yet. Nor could she tell them she had arranged to meet him at a coffee shop in town the next day.

Soon after, her father arrived home and walked into the kitchen.

"Lydia is upset. Sit down and listen to what happened."

"Lydia is upset?" He stared at his wife.

"Sit down."

Lydia told him the whole embarrassing tale about how she was rejected when she thought she was going to get married.

"What did you say his name was?"

"Caleb Glick," she said with a sigh. "It doesn't matter. I don't want to marry him.'

"And Paula said that's who Winston's sister is marrying," Sarah added. "Paula's gone over to Winston's *haus* now."

Their father asked, "And what does Paula think she can do about it?"

Lydia shook her head. "I don't know, but I hope it doesn't cause trouble between Paula and Winston."

Their mother stood up. "Dinner is only ten minutes away." That was their mother's way of telling everybody to get out of the kitchen and wash up, ready for dinner.

Lydia headed to her room, feeling embarrassed that everyone in the family knew she'd been rejected in the way that she had. She had intended to tell both of her sisters about the wonderful man she'd met, but now didn't seem the right time to do so.

LATER THAT NIGHT, after Paula came home, she went into Lydia's room and sat down on her bed.

"What happened?" Lydia asked.

"Winston's *vadder* said he'd have a talk with Caleb and sort it all out. Caleb's coming to their house tomorrow afternoon for a visit."

"*Ach nee.* I didn't want this."

"Well, I don't know what to say. He can't go around doing stuff like that."

"It's done and dusted. I'm okay and I don't want to marry him anymore."

"But you did, before you knew about Sally?"

"*Jah*, but now that I know, it's completely changed my opinion of him. I was only his backup plan."

"I'm going to bed."

"Okay, *gut nacht*."

"Night, Lydia."

"Oh, Paula?"

Paula stepped back into her bedroom. "*Jah?*"

"Are you going to see Winston tomorrow?"

"*Jah,* I see him every day after work."

"Can you tell his *vadder* it's all okay?"

"All right. If that's what you want."

"It is."

Paula walked away.

CHAPTER EIGHTEEN

The next day Lydia had arranged to meet Benjamin, but hadn't figured on it being one of Sarah's rare days off.

Lydia hurried to the coffee shop not liking to keep people waiting. It was all Sarah's fault for keeping her waiting because she had to take her to the stores.

When Lydia walked into the café, Benjamin stood up at his full height and waved to her. He must've been six-foot four inches or possibly even more. He looked even more handsome than she remembered and she hoped he wasn't disappointed when he saw her again. But from the way he was smiling, she guessed that he was pleased to see her.

"I'm sorry I'm late."

"I think I was early."

She laughed at him trying to be polite about it. "No, I'm definitely late, thanks to my little sister."

"What do you feel like drinking? Coffee or tea, or something else, and do you want something to eat?"

"Just coffee for me, thanks."

"I've been eyeing one of those chocolate cakes. Would you go halves with me on one of those?"

"I don't know if I could eat half. I could have a little bit of it, though."

"That sounds close enough to me."

He put his order in up at the counter while she patiently waited at the table with her back turned to him. Soon he was sitting in front of her again.

"It's so good to see you again, Lydia."

"It's nice to see you again, too. You look different somehow."

"I've let my hair grow a little just in case I come back to the community."

She gave a little giggle. "Are you truly thinking of it, or haven't you gotten around to getting a haircut."

He laughed. "You already know me too well. I haven't had time to get it cut with work being so busy. We've been doing one job after another, but I'm considering… Well, put it this way, I've given a fair bit of thought to coming back."

"Really?"

"Yes, it's true. It's always been in the back of my mind. It had never been my intention to stay away forever. How did you enjoy staying at your aunt's place?"

"It was good getting to know her with just me being there. Every other time I'd visited her, it was with the whole family. I've gotten to know her a lot better this time around, and she's not nearly as severe as I thought she was."

"I'm happy that you got that special time with her. You know, I remember that your parents used to live in a house near the bishop."

"Yes, that was the first house they lived in, when they first got married."

"Oh, now I'm showing my age. I don't like being so much older than you."

"Age is just a number, isn't it?" Lydia smiled at him, pleased that he also felt some sort of inadequacy.

"Yes, I like to think so."

The waitress brought over their coffees and a large piece of chocolate cake with a large dollop of fresh whipped cream."

"This looks incredible." Lydia resisted digging her fork into the creamy chocolate frosting.

"Did you tell your parents you were meeting me here today?"

"No, because I didn't see them much this morning. I'm not keeping it from them I just haven't got around to telling them yet. The story about Caleb was enough to start out with."

"I know your situation. You can't be friends with me, much less anything else, so that's why I'm thinking of returning."

"Coming back to the community?"

He nodded.

She stared into his blue-green eyes, wondering if it would ever really happen.

"I know there are many things to consider." He looked up at her and smiled. "Would you marry me if I came back to the community?"

She would in a heartbeat. "I don't think it's would be fair for me to answer that. I don't want to sway your decision."

"I wish you would, and then things would be so much easier for me."

Lydia took a sip of coffee.

"What are you doing with the rest of your day?" he asked when she didn't comment.

"My youngest sister is in town here somewhere, shopping. I am meeting her at the farmers market at three o'clock."

He glanced at his watch. "Three o'clock? That leaves us with a bit of time."

Lydia wanted to spin out their time together as much possible and if she had to do that by drinking one coffee after another until just before three, then that's exactly what she'd do. And that was what she did.

They finally had to part. At Benjamin's urging, Lydia agreed to call him the next day. Then Lydia hurried to collect Sarah.

That afternoon, Sarah and Lydia arrived home at the same time as their father. After they tended to the horses, they all walked into the house together.

Lydia's mother met them at the door looking worried. "Paula has come home in tears."

Sarah and Lydia looked at each other, wondering what to do.

"Where is she?" their father asked.

"Up in her room now. She's had some argument or other with Winston."

"Should I go up and see her?" Lydia asked her mother, who looked like she was white with shock.

Her mother nodded while Sarah just stood there.

Lydia walked up the stairs and opened her sister's door to see her crying into a pillow. She closed the door behind herself and then sat down on the bed. "What happened?"

Paula sat up. "Winston and I are through."

Lydia stomach churned. They were in love with each other, so how could things be over? "What happened?"

"When I got over there to his house, Winston's sister was there and Caleb was there. I asked him in front of everybody why he said he would marry you and then went back on it."

"In front of everybody?"

"*Jah,* and then he stuttered for a bit and said you must've misunderstood everything."

"That's not right and I've got the letters to prove it. He asked me to marry him and I said yes. He even arranged for me to stay at someone's house nearby until we got married."

"Don't worry, I knew you'd be telling the truth. Some people handle the truth loosely. And then Winston was trying to hush me. I will say what I have to say. I think it was wrong what Caleb did to you. He could've at least been respectful and told you he changed his mind or something and then waited a few months until he got engaged to Sally, but to do it right away, in backwards order, was terrible. And he had no regard for your feelings. It's not right, and I had to say so."

"I don't care about him anymore. I didn't want this to come in between you and Winston." This reinforced that she couldn't mention Benjamin—not just yet. Her sister had been protective of her and it had lost Paula the man she loved—hopefully only temporarily. "The whole thing is mixed up and horrible. I wish I had never gone to stay with Aunt Stella."

CHAPTER NINETEEN

"*D*on't worry about me and Winston. It wasn't meant to be."

"Every couple has disagreements. You'll sort things out with him."

"We've had arguments before and there's a lot of things we don't agree on."

"You love him though, don't you?"

"I thought I did, but he should have been on my side and not his *schweschder's* side."

"Everyone's got their own opinion. And something like this doesn't necessarily have a side."

Paula looked at her with red-rimmed eyes. "I'd really rather be alone, Lydia."

"I'll bring dinner up to you when it's ready."

Paula shook her head. "I'm not hungry."

"Come into my room later if you want to talk."

Paula nodded. "Thanks, Lydia. I'm glad you're back home."

Lydia leaned over and kissed Paula on the forehead. "I'm glad to be home. Good night."

Just before dinner was ready, Paula had cheered up and was downstairs when Sarah ran into the living room from the kitchen. "There's a buggy coming to the *haus.*"

Everyone looked out the window, and when it came closer, *Mamm* said, "It's Winston."

"He's come to say he's sorry," Sarah said.

"Let's not jump to conclusions," their mother said.

Paula wiped her eyes and smoothed down her dress. "Do I look all right?"

"You don't look like you've been crying," Sarah said. "Well, you do a bit because your eyes are a little bit red."

Paula walked out the door, and Lydia and their mother and Sarah walked into the kitchen just in case Paula and Winston came back into the house.

"I reckon he's come here to apologize."

Lydia said, "There might not be anything to apologize for. But it's a good sign that he's come here to talk." That eased Lydia's conscience a lot.

When they heard the buggy leaving half an hour later, they headed to the front door and waited to see what had happened.

Paula looked much better and she was even smiling. "What happened?" their mother asked.

"Winston's father had a talk with Caleb for a few hours last night, and Caleb realized that what he did was wrong and then Caleb said he'll marry you now, Lydia."

Mamm and Sarah stared at Paula.

"What about Winston sister?"

"I just told them what you told me. She only wanted to marry Caleb when she found out you were marrying him."

"I need to sit down."

Paula followed her to the couch and sat next to her. "Caleb's coming here tonight to sort things out with you and make things right."

Lydia swallowed hard. She was sure she had told Paula that she didn't like this man. "I told you that I didn't like him when I met him."

"Before or after he told you that he was marrying someone else?"

"After, I think it was, because I had made the commitment to marry him. But not af- ter... not after I found out what kind of a person he was."

Her mother sat down on the other side of her. "I would say he's a very good kind of a man if he's trying to make things right. Right his wrongs. It takes a lot for someone to do that."

"Yes, and Winston's sister was sneaky because she only wanted him when she knew you wanted him."

Lydia put her elbows on her knees and leaned over and cradled her face. This was turning out dreadfully, and she could only imagine how upset Winston's sister was.

"You don't look happy, Lydia."

"This wasn't how I wanted things to go."

"You wanted to get married, that's why you went to Aunt Stella's. Aunt Stella found this man for you and now you are rejecting him just because of one mistake that he made?" their mother asked.

"Not exactly. Right away when I saw him I realized he hadn't been honest in his letters to me. Then I turned off of him completely when he told me he was marrying someone else. Why should I take him back? I don't want to be someone's second-best. I can't marry him. Not knowing he really wanted to marry Sally."

Paula leaped to her feet. "After all I've done for you? Winston and I are still barely talking to each other."

"I didn't ask you to go over there, Paula. In fact, I tried to stop you."

Paula sat back down. "I've just made things worse, haven't I?"

"Maybe. I don't know what to say to him when he comes here tonight. How is Winston's sister handling the news?"

"I think she's fine. Now that her father has pointed out that he made the agreement to marry you first. Winston's father can be very convincing."

"I'll sort things out with him tonight."

When Lydia's father came downstairs,

everyone talked at once about Caleb and Winston's father coming to the house.

"Slow down. I can only listen to one person at a time." He sat down on the couch. "Now tell me who's coming to the *haus?*"

"Winston's father is coming here with Caleb tonight, and they want to talk to you, *Dat*. About how Caleb treated Lydia," Paula said.

"What does this mean?" he asked.

"They just want to make sure everything is done properly. I'd say that's what it is."

"They might ask you if you want to marry him," their father said to Lydia.

"I'll just say no and be done with it."

"That will make Paula look bad in front of Winston's *vadder*," *Mamm* pointed out.

Lydia frowned at her mother. "I can't marry the man if I don't like him, *Mamm*."

"I'm not saying that. I'm just saying it's not doing Paula much good."

"That's why I wish I had never gone over," Paula said.

"Don't worry. Everything will work out. The Word says that all things work together for good."

"I hope so," their mother muttered. "We should eat dinner now, before they arrive."

CHAPTER TWENTY

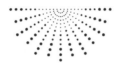

*L*ydia was nervous about seeing Caleb again. However, she didn't want to seem that way at all. He had seemed nice in his letters, but someone nice would not do what he had done to her. It was shameful and embarrassing, and now this whole thing was all blown out of proportion. She would simply have to tell him that he could marry Winston's older sister. It didn't help Lydia's confidence very much that Sally was a couple of years younger, and she was prettier, and, of course, smaller. But,

Lydia reminded herself if she married a big tall man like Benjamin, her size wouldn't be such an issue.

At eight o'clock Lydia's mother let everybody into the house and showed them into the living room, and then she and Paula and Sarah disappeared into the kitchen. Lydia was left with her father, and Caleb, who barely made eye contact with her, and then there was Winston and Sally's father, Peter Yoder.

Lydia had a chance to study Caleb because she was sitting on one couch next to her father, with the other two men sitting across from them. He looked nervous and, by the way his eyes darted around the room, Lydia was sure he was put off by her physical appearance.

"Let's get down to the reason we're here," Peter Yoder said.

"I owe you an apology, Lydia," Caleb said, now looking straight at her for the very first time since he stepped foot in the house.

"I believe we've already said all we had to say, at the train station that day."

"I asked you to marry me, and you said yes, so I have withdrawn my offer of marriage from Sally Yoder because my engagement to you was agreed upon first."

Lydia stared into his cold eyes. He'd obviously memorized that speech and didn't mean a word of it. Sure, he might've intended to carry out marrying her, but the two of them would never be in love. Lydia opened her mouth, about to tell him that it was perfectly all right with her if he married Sally, that she would be fine with it and there would be no hard feelings, but she didn't get a chance.

"That's what I came here to say tonight, but there is this other component to this story that you should be aware of, both of you, Mr. Yoder and Mr. Raber." He looked directly at both men in turn. "I don't think that Lydia here is the slightest bit interested in me because she has been secretly dating an *Englischer.*"

Lydia froze in place and didn't know what to do or where to look so she looked at the floor.

"Now just a moment, Caleb, my *dochder* would not do such a thing. She hasn't got a deceptive bone in her body. I don't think you've gone about things in a very good way. If you're not willing to marry her you should just say so and be a man about it."

Lydia couldn't go on another moment letting her father defend her.

"*Dat,* I do have a friend who is an *Englischer.*" She looked at Caleb. "Are you talking about Benjamin Dawson?"

"That's exactly who I'm talking about, and let me tell you, Mr. Raber, they are more than friends."

"I am aware of the friendship. Lydia told

me that she met Benjamin and we used to know him and his family from the community. I repeat what I said before, Caleb; if you don't want to marry my daughter you should just say so, but none of this matters because I won't allow her to marry you."

Peter Yoder leaned forward. "Now, let's just calm down. There's no need for anyone to get excited."

"I'm calm," her father said. "And I'll calmly not allow Lydia to marry this man."

Caleb sprang to his feet. "I don't think I'm welcome here, Mr. Yoder. I think Mr. Raber wants Lydia to marry a man from her own community."

Her father stood. "I do appreciate you both coming here and trying to sort this out but this is a situation that can't be sorted. And I think as far as Lydia is concerned, your daughter can marry Caleb, Peter. Wouldn't that be right, Lydia?"

Lydia nodded. "I don't mind who Caleb marries. But it won't be me."

"I'm happy we were able to sort things out here tonight," Peter Yoder said. No one responded.

Lydia sat frozen to the couch while her father showed them to the door. She was pleased her father was totally on her side, but when he had closed the door, he walked into the living room and looked at her.

"Exactly how close are you to Benjamin Dawson?" He folded his arms and stared at her.

"Um, it's hard to say."

"Is what Caleb said true?"

"I like him a lot."

"And is that why you won't marry Caleb?"

"Nee. I won't marry Caleb because he didn't stick to his word, and he didn't care about me at all. It was so horrible, and Benjamin was there."

"Benjamin was where?"

Lydia drew in a long breath and exhaled. "Caleb had Benjamin drive him to the station in his car because it was too far to go by buggy from his house and he didn't want to pay for a taxi. He didn't even tell Benjamin why he was going to the station until he got back into the car after telling me he was marrying Sally instead of me. And Benjamin promptly told him to find his own way home. And then Benjamin came into the station to find me."

"And you never met him before that?"

Lydia shook her head vigorously. *"Nee, Dat.* I never even heard of his name before. I was too young when he was still in the community. He was so nice to me. He walked me to a place I could stay overnight, and then we had dinner together."

She could tell her father didn't like that part. His face screwed up and his dark eyebrows drew together. She knew she couldn't tell him that they spent the day together after that, or even that they'd met that very day at a coffee shop.

"*Denke, Dat*, for everything you said. It could've been awkward and embarrassing. Well, even more embarrassing."

"That's how it was for me," her father said. After staring at her, he walked outside and closed the door behind him.

That's just what he did whenever he had a lot on his mind or was worried about something. He always walked outside even when it was in the dark.

Lydia felt bad that she'd embarrassed her father, and went to find her mother in the kitchen. When she walked into the kitchen, she knew by the looks on her mother's and her sisters' faces, that they had heard everything that had taken place.

"Why didn't you tell us you liked Benjamin?" Paula asked.

"I was going to. But everything's just happen so quickly since I got home. I'm going up to my room. I feel awful about everything."

"Don't feel awful, Lydia. You don't have to marry Caleb anymore," Sarah said.

Lydia smiled. "I guess that's true."

"And Winston and I will be all right; we often argue about things... and then he realizes he was wrong," said Paula with a wink.

Lydia gave a little giggle. *"Gut nacht,* everyone."

Everyone said good night, and she headed up to her room. She was so glad that the horrible encounter was over. Sally would be pleased that she was free to marry Caleb. It was hard to believe that Caleb had blurted out in front of everyone that she was dating Benjamin. They were only in the friend stage. It just showed once again the type of man that Caleb was. She realized she'd had a lucky escape, thanks to Sally.

CHAPTER TWENTY-ONE

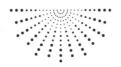

When Lydia woke up, she knew things couldn't carry on the same with Benjamin. Now people, including her own family, would be alert to her slipping away to meet him. She'd have to make a clean break from him, and hope that he'd return to the community one day. If he did, then they might have a chance at having a proper relationship.

She called his cell phone and arranged to meet him in town on Saturday.

Saturday came, and everyone in the family

went their separate ways. *Dat* went to work as usual and *Mamm* had her quilting bee, while her two sisters would be working. She'd offered to drive her sisters to work, and that way she'd have use of the buggy. Lydia had arranged to meet Benjamin at a park close to town.

When she pulled up the buggy, she saw his car was already parked and waiting. She stopped the buggy and heard his car door open. She glanced over and her heart filled with happiness when she saw his smiling face. He walked toward her and held her hand as she jumped down from the buggy.

"I'm glad you called."

"Good."

"Let's walk."

"Okay."

He put his hands in his pockets. "I've been doing a lot of thinking and I think we have to stop seeing each other and talking together."

"I know. That's what I wanted to talk to you about."

He stopped walking. "What?"

"It's best," she said, now staring up into his face.

"Stop seeing each other only for a few weeks, because I'm coming back to the community. I meant just until I get settled somewhere."

"You mean it?"

"Yes."

"I can't believe it."

He chuckled. "I'm glad you're pleased. You had me worried there. I have this picture in my mind and it's a lovely scene."

He took her arm and led her to a wooden seat.

"Tell me about this scene."

"Well, there's you, and then there's me. There's this nice little house, and we live in it together as man and wife."

She giggled, pleased that everything seemed to be turning out to suit her.

"As soon as it's right, I'll come back to you once I'm settled back into the community and I'll ask you to marry me."

Lydia stared at him, lost for words.

"I figure we'll be married in a few months. I'm a man of action. Once I've made up my mind about something, I don't waste any time. Don't answer my proposal just yet; I'll ask again when I'm baptized and as soon as the bishop allows." He tipped his head slightly, not taking his eyes from her. "Would you say yes if all those conditions were met?"

She smiled and nodded.

He took hold of her hand. "I can't tell you how happy that makes me. You've changed my life, Lydia Raber."

"And you've changed mine."

"I'll never give you cause to be disappointed in me. I'll be a good husband."

"I'll try to be a good wife."

"Now, I'll let you in on a small secret."

"Oh no! What is it? I usually don't like secrets."

"I'm getting baptized on Sunday."

"What? That's only a few days time."

"I know."

"It's hard to believe this is happening. How did you do this all so fast?"

"I told you I like things to move quickly. We both deserve happiness."

Lydia nodded as she looked away from him across the green fields, which made up the park. For the longest time she had thought she didn't deserve happiness, but now she knew that happiness was no longer out of her reach.

"What are you thinking?"

She looked back at him. "I'm thinking I'm so glad I met you that day at the station. It was the lowest day of my life, and also the best."

"I want to make sure that every day from

now on is your best day."

"That sounds *wunderbaar.*"

"I'm looking forward to meeting your parents. Again, I should say. I hope they don't think I'm too old for you."

"They'll be okay. They only had good things to say about you."

"Really?"

"*Jah.* I asked them if they remembered you, and they did."

"Well, that's a worry off my mind. Why don't you come and have a quick look at my house right now? We can live there after we marry. I bought it only a year ago and it's not too far away from where a lot of the folk in the community live."

"I don't want to leave the horse. Can we take him instead of the car?"

"Yeah, it's not far."

"Okay." They both walked back to the buggy.

"It's been a long time since I've been in one of these. I've missed driving a buggy."

"How will you adjust?"

"No problem at all."

"Do you want to drive?"

"Yes, why not."

They swapped places and Benjamin drove to his house with Lydia beside him. She looked over at him driving the buggy and felt that everything about him was perfect.

When she stepped out onto the property, Lydia was amazed at how pretty the quaint little cottage looked from the outside. It was wonderful, and with her womanly touch, it would be perfect. He was right about it being the perfect home for a child, or better yet, for a family. She couldn't wait to write to Aunt Stella to tell her that she'd gotten a good and kind man, and that if it weren't for her help, she never would've found him.

Before following him inside, Lydia stood

at the bottom of the front steps and looked up. Closing her eyes briefly, she said a silent prayer to thank God for them meeting.

JUST LIKE BENJAMIN HAD SAID, he got baptized at the next Sunday meeting. When the meeting ended, everyone was fussing around him while Lydia listened nearby. One man was offering to accompany him to buy a horse and buggy while others were inviting him for dinner. It made Lydia happy that they were all warm and accepting.

When everyone was starting to leave, Benjamin walked over to her.

"You're very popular today."

"I doubt it will last. Anyway, as long as I'm popular with you that's all I care about."

"Tom seemed keen to help you buy a buggy."

"I've already done that and I'm picking it up tomorrow, as well as my new horse."

"That was fast. Are you still coming for dinner tomorrow night?"

"I sure am."

"Good. How are you feeling about everything?"

He smoothed back his hair, which was still a little damp. "I'm feeling… like I can't describe how I'm feeling. I'm pleased to be back. It's right. This is my home."

She heard running footsteps behind her, and then someone tugged on her arm. Turning around she saw that it was Sarah.

"Mamm says to ask Benjamin if he wants us to drive him home."

Smiling, pleased that her parents liked him, she asked, "Well?"

"Jah, that would be good."

"They said they're ready to go when you are," Sarah said.

"Tell them I'll just have a quick word with

the bishop and then I'll meet you at the buggy."

Lydia and Benjamin exchanged smiles before Lydia walked with Sarah to the family buggy.

"He's in love with you," Sarah whispered.

"Do you think so?"

Sarah dug her in the ribs. "You know he is. That's why he's here. Everyone knows it."

"Everyone?"

"Well, just me and Paula. And I know how you feel about him. I'm happy for you."

TWO MONTHS LATER, Lydia and Benjamin stood before the bishop. Lydia was wearing a blue dress that Aunt Stella had made for her. Benjamin had asked her so many times to marry him; it was nice that it was finally happening. While the bishop spoke on marriage as they stood before him, Lydia could barely keep the smile from her face. She was still a big woman, but *Gott* had found her a large man who loved her for herself. He was in every way her perfect match.

Later, when the wedding celebrations were coming to a close, Aunt Stella grabbed her hand, pulling her up from the table where she sat next to Benjamin.

"I've got something for you, Lydia."

"What is it?"

"Come and see. I've got it in the *haus*."

Lydia followed her aunt into her parents' house, and in the corner of the living room was a large package wrapped with brown paper and string.

"Open it," Stella said.

Lydia pulled on the string and Aunt Stella helped her pull the paper apart. When she saw the star quilt that she'd admired at Stella's *haus,* she couldn't believe her eyes. "Oh, Aunt Stella! It's your quilt."

"Now it's yours. I was going to sew you

another one exactly the same, but this one was used by your *vadder's mudder* and it's special. I want you to have it."

"*Denke.* It's so *wunderbaar.*" Lydia wiped a tear from her eye. "It *is* special. I love it so much, and it's so precious. It's got so much history attached to it, with your parents' *haus* burning down, and then you making this as a replica for the one your mother lost. I'll think of you and *Grossmammi* every time I see it."

Stella smiled. "I was hoping you'd like it. And remember *Grossmammi* got the first one on her wedding day. All the women in the *familye* had made it for her, and kept it a secret until the day. And now you've received this one on your wedding day."

"I love it. It's so thoughtful, Aunt Stella, *denke.*"

"Benjamin is a *gut* man. You'll be happy with him."

"I'm glad you like him."

"Everyone does," Stella said with a twinkle in her eyes.

"Just think, I never would've met him if I hadn't gone to your *haus,* and if you hadn't written those letters."

"*Jah,* you never would've traveled to Ephrata and then met Benjamin."

Lydia hugged the quilt and held it up to her face. "He's so perfect for me."

"*Gott* chose him for you, that's why. And He rewards those who add works to their faith and that's what you did when you came and stayed with me."

"*Denke* for everything, Aunt Stella. This quilt will be *wunderbaar* and it will look so good in the bedroom. Next time you visit, you'll have to stay with us."

Aunt Stella chuckled. "I will. Now you better get back to your husband. He'll be wondering why you've been away from him for so long."

Together Aunt Stella and Lydia went

back outside to the yard, where the wedding breakfast was being held.

Aunt Stella walked to her brother while Lydia walked over to her new husband, saying another silent prayer of thanks for Benjamin coming into her life.

When she sat down next to him, he looked at her and the corners of his mouth twitched with a smile. "Where have you been?"

"Aunt Stella gave us her beautiful star quilt. It's got a story attached to it. I'll tell you about it later."

"*Denke* for marrying me, Lydia. You've changed my life and made me the happiest man in the world. I never thought I'd find anyone like you—ever."

"*Gott* brought us together."

"You're a gift, Lydia. A gift from *Gott*."

When someone came up behind Benjamin and tapped him on the shoulder to talk to him, Lydia looked over at the house. There she saw Tiger, the old barn cat, lazing on the porch keeping a watch on the festivities. That jerked Lydia's memory back to the day she'd looked down on her sister and Winston from her bedroom window. She'd been envious of the love that the two of them shared. Immediately she had been able to push those futile thoughts away, and then she'd prayed that she'd someday look at a man the way her sister had looked at Winston. God had answered that prayer and all the others. Not only had she found that man, but now they were married. And she was the first of her sisters to marry just like she'd secretly hoped.

Now Lydia was free of the burden that she was a large woman. Next to Benjamin, she *was* the perfect size and he loved everything about her, just the way she was.

And be not conformed to this world: but be ye transformed by the renewing of your mind, that ye may prove what is that good, and acceptable, and perfect, will of God.
Romans 12:2

Thank you for reading The Amish Spinster.

www.SamanthaPriceAuthor.com

THE NEXT BOOK IN THE
SERIES

Book 3:
The Amish Bishop's Daughter

When you're the bishop's daughter,
there are certain standards that have
to be met. Anna Weaver felt the
weight of that burden. Believing
people were always waiting for her to
put a foot wrong, she retreated into
her shell and had few friends. There
was only one man she did not feel
awkward around, and that was her

close friend, Levi Glick. Even though he had been in and out of the Amish community over the past year, Anna was certain he would soon commit to the Amish faith by baptism, and she ignored the rumors about him.

AMISH MISFITS

Book 1 The Amish Girl Who Never Belonged

Book 2 The Amish Spinster

Book 3 The Amish Bishop's Daughter

Book 4 The Amish Single Mother

Book 5 The Temporary Amish Nanny

Book 6 Jeremiah's Daughter

Book 7 My Brother's Keeper

Book 8 The Amish Marriage Pact

ALL SAMANTHA PRICE'S SERIES

Amish Maids Trilogy
A 3 book Amish romance series of novels featuring 5 friends finding love.

Amish Love Blooms
A 6 book Amish romance series of novels about four sisters and their cousins.

Amish Misfits
A series of 7 stand-alone books about people who have never fitted in.

The Amish Bonnet Sisters
To date there are 28 books in this continuing family saga. My most popular and best-selling series.

Amish Women of Pleasant Valley
An 8 book Amish romance series with the same characters. This has been one of my most popular series.

Ettie Smith Amish Mysteries
An ongoing cozy mystery series with octo-genarian sleuths. Popular with lovers of mysteries such as Miss Marple or Murder She Wrote.

Amish Secret Widows' Society
A ten novella mystery/romance series - a prequel to the Ettie Smith Amish Mysteries.

Expectant Amish Widows

A stand-alone Amish romance series of 19 books.

Seven Amish Bachelors
A 7 book Amish Romance series following the Fuller brothers' journey to finding love.

Amish Foster Girls
A 4 book Amish romance series with the same characters who have been fostered to an Amish family.

Amish Brides
An Amish historical romance. 5 book series with the same characters who have arrived in America to start their new life.

Amish Romance Secrets
The first series I ever wrote. 6 novellas following the same characters.

Amish Christmas Books

Each year I write an Amish Christmas stand-alone romance novel.

Amish Twin Hearts
A 4 book Amish Romance featuring twins and their friends.

Amish Wedding Season
The second series I wrote. It has the same characters throughout the 5 books.

Amish Baby Collection
Sweet Amish Romance series of 6 stand-alone novellas.

Gretel Koch Jewel Thief
A clean 5 book suspense/mystery series about a jewel thief who has agreed to consult with the FBI.

Made in United States
Orlando, FL
19 July 2023

35267473R00134